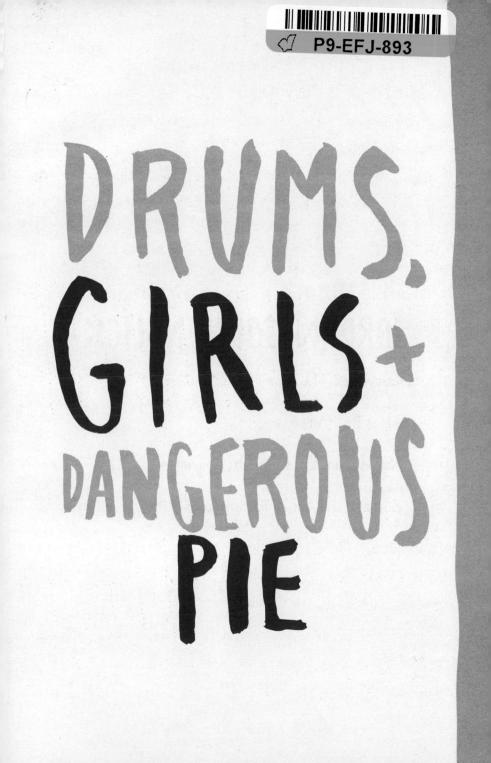

DRUMS, GIRLS + DANGEROUS PIE

JORDAN SONNENBLICK

DRUMS, GIRLS + DANGEROUS PIE

SCHOLASTIC INC.

This book was originally published in hardcover by Scholastic Press.

ISBN 978-0-545-72286-5

28 27 26 25 24   19/0

Printed in the U.S.A.   40
This edition first printing, May 2014

The text type was set in Gill Sans.
The display type was hand-lettered by Nina Goffi.
Book design by Nina Goffi and Marijka Kostiw

ACKNOWLEDGMENTS

You don't hear enough good things about the New York City public schools. The following New York City teachers were all crucial to my development as a writer: Mrs. Gross, my first-grade teacher at P.S. 35, who started me out right; Miss Tuff, my fourth-grade teacher at P.S. 54, who let me be creative; Mrs. Palma, my seventh-grade English teacher at I.S. 61, who made me write in a journal every day; Dr. Bindman, my tenth-grade English teacher at Stuyvesant High School, who taught me how to analyze the structure of a novel; and Frank McCourt, who told me I was a born writer and somehow made me believe it.

Three other New York teachers, through their own authorship, passed writing down to me as a legacy: my aunt, Ida Meltzer; my grandfather, Sol Feldman; and my mother, Dr. Carol Sonnenblick. I thank them for leading the way.

Special mention goes to my best friend's mom, Joan Gattullo, who was the very first person who told me I would write a book someday.

During the actual writing of this book, several people lifted me up and carried me along. I owe endless thanks to my wife and eternal first reader, Melissa; my children, Ross and Emma, who had to share Daddy with a computer screen; my cancer-research guru, Dr. Benjamin Purow; the authors Paula Cohen and David Lubar, who lent a hand to a new guy; my teaching colleague Marlene Sharpe, who was never too busy to listen; and the best early readers a writer could wish for: the Hornungs; the Winchels; my father, Dr. Harvey Sonnenblick; Adam Pines; Mark Chou; Matt Lambiase; Samantha Cattaneo; Karen Skalitzky; and the brave members of the Phillipsburg Middle School Literary Society, who stayed after school to read the first draft of this book.

Finally, thanks to everyone at DayBue Publishing for giving a new writer a wonderful opportunity; to my excellent agent, Rich Barber, for leaping into the breach; and to the great people at Scholastic for taking my dream to a whole new level.

TABLE OF CONTENTS

DANGEROUS PIE

There's a beautiful girl to my left, another to my right. Hundreds of colored balloons are tethered down behind me, baking in the June sun. I'm wearing a brown gown that's sticking to my sweat-drenched skin, trying to keep my head straight so that my weird square cap doesn't fall off in front of the thousand people who are watching me. And of course, because I'm me, I'm spacing out. The questions are just tumbling through my mind.

"How did I get up here? What have I learned since September? How could my life have possibly changed so much in only ten months?"

I'm not even sure I understand the questions, much less where to begin looking for the answers.

I guess a good starting point would be the longest journal I've ever written in English class. This was back in September, when I was pretty sure about life. The topic was "The most annoying thing in the world," and we were supposed to write the usual one-page response to it. I sat there for a few minutes, staring at the back of Renee Albert, who's the hottest girl in the eighth grade, trying to concentrate. Unfortunately, all I could concentrate on was Renee Albert. Did I mention she's the hottest girl in the eighth grade? Miss Palma is always going on and on about brainstorming and lists and "prewriting," so I started a list of truly annoying things:

- Journal assignments
- Dull pencils
- The pencil sharpener smell
- Miss Palma's perfume
- Why doesn't Renee Albert ever look at me?
- Hot girls who never look at skinny geeks
- Being a skinny geek
- Being a skinny geek named Steven

Just then I realized that Miss Palma was standing behind me, reading over my shoulder (I guess that's why I was being asphyxiated by her perfume).

Thinking fast, I covered up my list, turned to her,

and asked, *Miss Palma, can the journal be longer than a page?*

Sure, Steven. Why? What are you thinking about creating here?

("Creating here." She actually said that. Don't English teachers just slay you? My mom is actually an English teacher, but that doesn't mean I don't find my own English teachers a bit odd.)

Well, I'm having trouble crafting my prose.

(Yeah, "crafting my prose." Two can play this game. . . .)

What's your topic? Remember what I always say: "F. F. F!"

(Stands for "Form Follows Function," don't ya know.)

Ummm . . . I want to write about a big topic. And it's not exactly a thing. It's . . . it's . . .

(And then it hit me. The most annoying thing in my world is . . .)

My little brother, Jeffrey.

Wow, that's an ambitious topic! Go ahead. If you

need extra time, feel free to take the project home tonight, as well.

Thanks, Miss Palma. A lot.

Anyway, here's what I wrote:

Having a brother is horrible. Having any brother would be horrible, I suppose, but having my particular brother, Jeffrey, is an unrelenting nightmare. It's not because he's eight years younger than I am, although that's part of it. How would you like to be King of the Planet for eight glorious years, and then suddenly get demoted to Vice-King? It's not because he's cuter than I am, although that's part of it, too. I have mouse-brown cowlick-y hair, glasses that are about an inch thick, and braces that look like I tried to swallow a train wreck. He has those perfect little-kid Chiclet-white teeth, 20-20 vision, and little blond ringlets like the ones on the angels you see on the posters in art class. It's not even because he hates me — he doesn't. The truth is that he idolizes me. And that's the problem: The kid follows me around like I'm Elvis or something. And while he's being much too cute and following me around, he also destroys all of my stuff, including my self-esteem and my sanity.

Take, for example, the "Dangerous Pie" incident. Jeffrey has known from an early age that the worst possible thing he can do to me is to touch my drum stuff. I have some rules about this: He may not PLAY the drums, he may not pretend the cymbals are shields and he is a knight, he may not hide IN the bass drum, and pretty much any Jeffrey-to-drumsticks contact is a massive no-no. But on one fateful afternoon last year, Jeffrey threw the rules out the window.

On the tragic day, I came home, said hi to Mom, glugged down some milk, and headed down to the basement to practice. I was in a particularly good mood, I remember, because Renee Albert had told me in P.M. homeroom that she liked my shirt. As this was such a grand occasion, I decided to take the Special Sticks down from their sacred perch and use them for my practice-pad warm-up. In case you didn't know this, a practice pad is a thick, dense, flat piece of rubber. Usually it's glued onto a piece of wood.

You practice playing drums on it, because it feels a lot like playing on a real drumhead. Anyhow, the Special Sticks would be just an ordinary pair of my favorite sticks — Regal Tip 5A's with nylon tips — except that they have been autographed by my all-time drum hero, Carter Beauford of the Dave Matthews Band. I once saved up all my babysitting money for a couple of months, got two tickets to a drum clinic Carter Beauford was giving an hour and a half away in Philadelphia, and begged my dad to take me for two weeks until he finally gave in. At the clinic, during what I like to think of as the Two Glorious Minutes, Carter Beauford himself called me up front to demonstrate a double-stroke roll. After I did it, he said I had "nice technique" and signed my sticks, right there in front of a roomful of drummers! So I had spent quite a bit of blood, toil, tears, and sweat in order to get the Special Sticks.

But the Special Sticks weren't on their shelf.

Jeffrey!

I ran upstairs at top speed, hoping I would be in time but knowing that the odds were stacked against me. I burst into the kitchen and found Jeffrey doing his "cooking" thing on the floor. Pots and pans were everywhere — don't ask me how I had somehow not noticed this on my way downstairs the first time — and Jeffrey was stirring some pretend concoction in the deepest pot of all. With my Special Sticks.

I advanced toward him, with what must have been a disturbing gleam of violence in my eye.

Jeffrey! Give-me-the-sticks!

But I'm just COOKING.

Give-me-the-sticks!

But the Dangerous Pie isn't READY yet.

I don't care about your stupid four-year-old make-believe food. Give-me-the-sticks!

But this is REAL food!

And it was. Jeffrey's "Dangerous Pie" was a zesty blend of coffee grounds, raw eggs and their smashed shells, Coke, uncooked bacon, and three Matchbox racing cars.

The Special Sticks STILL smell funny.

Or maybe I should tell you about the "Please

kill me, Mom" affair. This fiasco happened after my All-City High School Jazz Band concert last June. Getting into the All-City band is a big, big deal, especially for a drummer — because there are six trumpeters, five saxes, four trombones, et cetera, but only two drummers. It was even a bigger deal for me last year, because I was the first seventh-grade drummer EVER admitted into the All-City high school band. They even had to send a special van to the middle school just to get me and this girl named Annette Watson, who's the backup piano player. She's actually really good, but there's this twelfth-grade guy who's been the main pianist since he was a freshman, and he's not about to get booted by a middle school girl in his senior year. She's funny, and she may be the only kid in the middle school who cares about music the way I do, but she's also kind of weird. It's like she's figured out how to play Beethoven and Thelonious Monk but hasn't quite mastered the art of being a girl yet.

It's not easy being the youngest guy in the band, by the way. They make fun of me all the time about my age, my size, my braces, and the way I stick out my tongue when I play. Also, everyone in the band has a cool nickname. When I first found this out at a rehearsal, the other drummer, Brian, was telling me what to call all the different people:

Who's that?

That's the King.

Who's he?

The Duke.

Who's she?

The Princess.

What do they call you?

The Count.

What does that make me?

Umm . . . how about the Peasant?

And the name stuck.

Anyway, my whole family came to the concert, and it was AWESOME. I had this huge drum feature in this Brian Setzer song called "Jump Jive an' Wail," and I nailed the whole thing. I usually practice at least an hour a day on my practice pad and another half hour on my drum set, plus I play in the marching band and the jazz group in school, AND we had been rehearsing twice a week for All-City for a couple of months, AND I used to take lessons once a week, so I was playing great that night. So after the concert, my parents and Jeffrey came to the band room. They were all excited and everything, but Jeffrey was bouncing off the ceiling.

You're a rock star, Steven.

No, I'm a JAZZ star, Jeffrey.

MY BROTHER IS A ROCK STAR! MY BROTHER IS A ROCK STAR!

Just then, Renee Albert stopped right next to us to congratulate her boyfriend (we'll just call him Biff), a sophomore guitarist with an alarmingly perfect complexion and muscles like Barry Bonds. Jeffrey saw Renee and started to whirl toward her — she lives around the corner from us, and I guess not even four-year-olds are immune to her charms and wiles. It seemed to happen in slow motion; events were just crawling. Yet still, I knew I would never have time to run across town to the local zoo, steal an elephant tranquilizer gun, run back, and fire it into Jeffrey's buttock before he could blurt out something that would mortify me and destroy my social status forever.

Life snapped back into full speed, and Jeffrey shouted: *Hey, Renee! MY BROTHER IS A ROCK STAR!*

As Biff looked on with a sneer, Renee replied, *Oh, really? I didn't know that.*

Yup, he IS. Did you SEE him? His arms were ZOOM-ING around the drums. Just like when he practices at home in front of the MIRROR.

Steven . . . ummm . . . practices in front of a mirror?

Yeah, it's COOL. In his UNDERWEAR. The BLUE ones! Right, Steven?

I sagged against my mom's shoulder and muttered, *Please kill me, Mom.*

My dad tried at that point to control the situation, but by now Jeffrey had drawn a little crowd of my bandmates, who were just waiting to see what else he would reveal about the Peasant.

My brother's GREAT! Hey, Renee, do you want to hear a JOKE? What does I-C-U-P spell?

I give up.

Close the bathroom door! GET IT?

I tried to end this torment. *Come on, Jeff. It's time to go out for ice cream with Mom and Dad.*

Just then Brian chimed in (he had dropped a stick during "In the Mood," and may have been annoyed by the big applause after my solo). *Let him finish, Peasant.*

To which Renee and my mom simultaneously turned to me and burst out, *They call you PEASANT?*

Dear Reader: Are you starting to see a pattern here?

• • •

Miss Palma gave me an A on the journal entry — she called it "droll" — so I guess I actually managed to get some use out of Jeffrey's antics before the chaos of this year started. Looking back on those days now, I'd have *eaten* the Dangerous Pie if I could have stopped October from coming.

JEFFREY'S MOATMEAL ACCIDENT

If I live to be a hundred and seventy-nine, I will never forget October 7th of this year. Oh, I'll try. I've been trying already. But I will never be able to throw off the weight of this particular day.

The weird thing is, the day started off great. I recall that I woke up early, for some reason, and couldn't go back to sleep. So I got out of bed, tiptoed to the bathroom, peed, and did my usual slow-motion Ninja walk to get down our squeaky stairs without waking up the 'rents or Jeffrey. I stopped in the kitchen to suck down some OJ, and then continued my silent journey to the basement. My dad has a separate little office down there. He's an accountant, and because he sometimes works really late hours during tax season, he had the walls filled with extra insulation for warmth and soundproofing. I figured I'd get some practice in on the pad before school, so I set myself up in the office. I started to work my way through my usual warm-up routine — five minutes of single-stroke rolls (right-left-right-left), five minutes of double-stroke rolls (right-right-left-left), and five minutes of paradiddles (right-left-right-right, left-right-left-left). My hands were feeling particularly loose, and somehow it was nice being up before anyone else, doing my own thing. Which, of course, meant that Jeffrey was bound to find me.

Steven!

Yaaaggghhh! You almost gave me a heart attack, you little madman.

(This made him giggle hysterically, as it always does when I pretend he's snuck up on me. But today he really HAD snuck up on me; my drumming concentration can be pretty fierce).

Steven, I don't feel good.

Lately, Jeffrey had been complaining a lot that his "parts hurt," which we hadn't been understanding too well. I thought it was just another one of his little-kid things, like the summer he turned three, when he convinced himself that he slept with his eyes open. I spent weeks trying to convince him that he slept with his eyes closed, just like everyone else on the planet. I finally videotaped about fifteen minutes of him sleeping, which I thought would settle the issue. When I played the tape back for him, though, he insisted, "Of course my eyes close SOMETIMES when I sleep. That's just what we call a slow blink."

So you can see why nobody was running outside to flag down an ambulance when this kid's "parts hurt."

What do you want me to do?

Can you make me some moatmeal?

Some oatmeal?

Right. Some moatmeal.

Jeff, gimme a break. I'm practicing here.

But I'm cold. I need moatmeal to warm up my parts.

I could see I wasn't going to get out of this one without a fight, and I am a pretty big oatmeal fan myself to tell you the truth. However, I couldn't resist teasing Jeffrey a little, so I said:

Cream of wheat.

Moatmeal.

Cream of wheat.

MOATMEAL.

Cream of wheat.

MOATMEAL!

Okay, you don't have to call out the National Guard. I'll make the oatmeal.

Yay! Moatmeal!

Up in the kitchen, I sat Jeffrey on a bar stool so he could "help" by mixing the oatmeal with the water before I nuked it. My mom always tells me not to leave Jeffrey up on the high stools without me standing right next to him, but she's ridiculously overprotective. If she had her way, he'd be wearing body armor to kindergarten. Anyway, he was babbling away about how our "special moatmeal treat" would "refix" his "parts" when I turned away for a second to get a wooden spoon. I heard a swish, a crack, a thump, and a little whimper. When I looked back, I realized that Jeffrey must have slipped off the stool and banged his face on the counter. He looked up at me from the floor for that miserable split second little kids always take before the wailing starts, and I saw a drop of blood under his nose. Then two things happened at once: He started to scream like a banshee, and the drop of blood turned into a torrent.

I grabbed the hand towel off of the refrigerator handle and held it to Jeffrey's nose. He looked terrified in a way I hadn't seen him before, and he was still screaming. I found myself pulling him onto my lap, saying things to him over and over, like, *Hush, Jeffy* — I never call him that unless he's upset — *it's OK. You're all right.*

When this didn't stop his wailing, and I knew the 'rents were about to come flying into the room any minute, I started to get a bit impatient. *C'mon, Jeffrey! It's a little nosebleed, that's all. You've had a million nosebleeds before, right?*

No, I've had TWO nosebleeds before. The time you let me skateboard and —

Okay, two nosebleeds. But nosebleeds go away, Jeff. You're fine. Now stop shouting before Mom and Dad —

Steven! What have you done to your brother?

Doh! Too late . . .

Nothing, Mom. I was making him breakfast, and he fell off his stool.

He JUST fell off? There was no pushing?

No.

No shoving, Steven?

No.

Did you drop him, Steven?

No.

Was this one of your wrestling moves, Jeffrey?

Finally, my parents were getting past the interrogation phase, and dealing with the injured child — who, by the way, was still receiving first aid from his heroic, wronged brother.

NO, Mommy.

Did you really JUST fall, Jeffrey?

Why does everybody in my family talk in these dramatic CAPITAL LETTERS all the time? Why am I the only calm one?

You know what, Mom? I body-slammed him, OK? I decided it would be really fun to set a five-year-old on a bar stool at 6:42 a.m., take a running leap, and knock him down like we were trying out for the WWF. It worked great, too.

Son, don't be defensive with your mother!

Defensive, Dad? DEFENSIVE?

Now they had me sinking to their capital-letter level.

YES! Defensive!

And FRESH!

Thanks for chiming in, Mom.

This could have gone on for months or even years, in an unending round of guilt-trip Ping-Pong, except Jeffrey stopped us all in our tracks. *Mommy, it hurts.*

This came out muffled, and we must have looked confused. So Jeffrey pushed my hand with the towel out of the way. It was another one of these frozen moments that always seem to happen to me; we all just looked at the towel, and Jeffrey's nose, and the front of my pajama shirt. There was an unbelievable amount of blood!

Oh God, Jeffy.

Oh, my God.

Get my shoes, Steven. I'm taking your brother to the emergency room.

I'd never seen my mom take one of our injuries so seriously before.

Honey, do you want me to go with . . . ?

Ahem, Dad.

No, you take this one to school.

Great — for the crime of attempted breakfast-making, I got demoted from "beloved firstborn" to "this one."

So my mom grabbed Jeffrey off of my lap, put another towel to his face (this one with ice wrapped in it), somehow got her shoes, his winter coat, her jacket, keys, her cell phone, and her purse, and got almost to the front door, before Jeffrey had time to say, *Beppie!*

Go get your brother his blanket, Steven.

For once I went to get my brother something without saying a word about it.

When I gave it to him, and my mom opened the door, I got one last long look at his frightened face over my mom's shoulder. As she started down the driveway toward the car, I had this weird feeling that my brother was getting smaller and smaller.

My dad closed the door and told me to go get ready for school.

Dad, is he —

I'm sure he'll be fine, Steven. Noses bleed a lot. Go!

That's when I looked at the kitchen clock and saw that it was already 7:09. We had to be out the door in eleven minutes. So I went upstairs, tossed the bloody PJ shirt in the bathroom sink, took the world's fastest shower, combed my hair into some kind of shape, and hurled myself into jeans and a Sum 41 T-shirt. By 7:14, I was at the door.

Dad! I'm ready!

My dad appeared with the attaché case I'd bought him for Christmas two years ago — *Guess what, Dad? It's a REAL accountant briefcase, with a REAL pocket for your calculator* — and got into his coat without a word.

Dad, are you, uh, OK?

I never particularly noticed my dad's moods, but he was looking kind of pale and tense. I glanced over at the kitchen and noticed that he had cleaned up Jeffrey's blood from the floor, which couldn't have been fun.

Fine. Come.

Great! And now for a fun ride to school with Caveman Dad.

In the car, things were 100% silent until I couldn't stand it anymore. I put on the radio to WZZO, the rock station, and started playing drums on my legs along with the Rush song that was on. My dad reached out and turned off the radio, which was very unusual for him. Even though my mom has always been my big "drum fan," my dad had at least succeeded in tuning out my tapping (OK, he called it "pounding" and my teachers always referred to it as "banging") on hundreds of car rides before this one.

Sorry, Steven. He said this with a weak little "I'm sorry" smile. *I need to concentrate on the road right now.*

Another few minutes of that weird "we're ignoring a topic" silence brought us to my school.

Before I got out of the car, I turned toward my dad for one more bit of whatever comfort he could give. *Dad, is he . . .*

I told you, Steven. Noses bleed a lot. Noses . . . just . . . bleed a lot. Now get going!

When I got to my locker, Renee Albert said hi to me from about a foot away — her locker has always been next to mine — and I realized I hadn't brushed my teeth.

Perfect.

ANXIETY WITH TIC TACS

I don't know about any of you, but when I'm nervous about something, I tend to think about it all day, unless I come up with a complicated mental trick to distract me. And even then, I'm still actually thinking about the thing by NOT thinking about it, if that makes any sense. It's like, if someone came up to you and said, "All right, now whatever you do, DON'T think of the color red." You'd try to picture a different color or repeat a recipe over and over in your head or count to a hundred and fifty-nine, but somewhere in the back of your mind, you'd be going, "Yellow . . . orange . . . red . . . DOH! Three eggs, separated . . . five slices American cheese . . . red . . . DANG! One hundred seventeen . . . one hundred eighteen . . . look at Renee's red lipstick . . . ARGHH!"

And that's how my October 7th went. I worked mightily to think about anything other than Jeffrey's gushing nose, but the distractions were truly pointless. In homeroom, after I figured out that my breath was going to present a challenge, I looked in the pocket of my Trapper Keeper for my box of Tic Tacs, and found that it was about three-quarters full. I quickly popped in a Tic Tac (orange, which I'm not even sure helps your breath anyway) and ran off to first period — Miss Palma's class. I did all the usual take-out-your-notebook stuff but then became lost in my own little don't-think-about-Jeffrey world. I used a trick that is pretty powerful for me; I came up with a really complex math problem to solve in my head:

"A boy has a box of forty Tic Tacs, and the box is three-quarters full. The Tic Tacs need to last through an entire school day and a bus ride home. The school day has seven periods. Each period is forty-four minutes long, with three minutes for passing between classes. Additionally, there is a twenty-two-minute lunch period and a four-minute afternoon homeroom period. The bus ride takes fifteen minutes, including the wait for the bus, boarding, and the actual time in transit. If the boy wants to make his Tic Tacs last until he arrives at home, how many minutes must he wait between Tic Tacs?"

So while everybody else was writing whatever the day's journal was supposed to be, I was agonizing over the details of this math problem. "OK, there are HOW many three-minute passing times? Seven, not counting the one before lunch. So eight. Eight times three is twenty-four. Plus the time in class, which is forty-four minutes times seven ... ummm ... OK, that's three hundred and eight minutes right there. And lunch is another twenty-two minutes, plus the bus is, like, fifteen minutes ... WAIT! Do I have to eat Tic Tacs during class? Who cares about my breath when I'm alone at my desk? But there IS group work in some ..."

Steven! Would you like to read your journal entry aloud?

No, thank you, Miss Palma.

Steven, I know I phrased that as a question, but it was really a command.

Yes, but mine is ... ummm ... private.

Private, Steven?

Yes, Miss Palma.

PRIVATE, Steven?

Again with the capital letters?

Yes, private.

Through my haze of math and memory, I gradually noticed that the class was cracking up.

Steven, I respect privacy as much as the next teacher, but how private can your thoughts on this question BE?

Well . . . I . . .

As it turns out, the topic was "Should foreign languages be taught in middle school?"

Things like that happened all day. After math, just as I popped in my seventh Tic Tac, Renee Albert said to me, *Steven, you are so, like, out of it today. Are you suffering from some kind of traumatic head injury or something?*

Well, sort of.

Are you sort of recovering, or was it sort of an injury?

Both. My brother fell off a stool this morning, and . . .

Oh, sorry, Steven. I have to go talk to Jenna and Steph. Wait up!

While Renee was attractively speed-walking away, Annette suddenly appeared next to me. It wasn't the first time I noticed this — how Renee kind of swished around in a cloud of perfume, and Annette just popped up like some spastic hand puppet.

Steven, I heard about Jeffy. What happened?

Annette sometimes watches Jeffrey on weekends.

He fell, and . . .

Yeah, I heard you telling the PRINCESS that part.

Well, his head hit the counter in the kitchen, and his nose was bleeding.

A lot?

Yeah. My mom went charging out with him. They went to the emergency room, and now I'm going to be in trouble, but I didn't even do . . .

Is he OK? Was he really scared?

I don't know.

And the bell rang, which meant I'd be late to social studies, and Annette would be late to science. While Annette ran away down the empty hall, it suddenly hit me that I hadn't even thought about how Jeffrey was feeling. And I didn't really want to think too hard about it, because I knew he'd be terrified. Plus, now I had to go get a late pass, which probably meant I'd get a detention. So Jeffrey was getting me in trouble again, as usual.

The high point of my day was my drum lesson. We have this thing called Opportunity Period, or O.P. It's the last period of the day, and if you don't owe work in any of your classes or need tutoring or have detention, you get to do fun stuff. Most of the kids like to go to gym during O.P. — the track, the weight room, and the pool are all open, and you can play basketball or volleyball, too. But some go to art or choir. And, of course, every chance I get, I go to the band room. A few times a week, I used to get individual lessons on the drum set with the band teacher, Mr. Watras, during O.P. On this particular day, Mr. W. got called to the office for something, so I had about fifteen minutes to just play drums, with nobody else around. I started out with some simple beats. When my hands and feet started to loosen up, I switched over to this really complicated Latin rhythm I'd been working on. It took a lot of concentration to keep all four limbs moving independently of each other, which was perfect. It meant I wasn't thinking about Jeffy's fall or late passes or even Renee Albert. I was just playing.

After keeping the beat going for five minutes or so, I burst into a big solo. I always think of it that way: "Here comes Steven, bursting into his Big Solo. Watch those hands — they're too quick to follow. Holy cow, this kid is a magician!" Like there's a Monday Night Football commentator standing over my left shoulder. Anyway, I really was flying. I started with both hands doing a kind of shuffled march on the snare drum, pretty quietly. As I gradually got louder, I started flicking little quick shots at the high toms. Then I threw in some big "bombs" with my bass drum foot. Soon, I had an incredibly fast para-diddle going between my left hand and my right foot, while my left foot was keeping time on the hi-hat cymbals and my right hand was going back and forth between the ride cymbal and the floor tom.

The door opened, and I opened my eyes and looked up (I never open my eyes when I'm practicing by myself — my private teacher always used to say if you don't know where the drums are, you're probably playing the wrong instrument). Mr. W. was back. Behind him, I could see a few kids I didn't know — probably sixth graders on their way somewhere — looking in. They started clapping when I looked their way, which was pretty cool. I hadn't been showing off on purpose, but I can't say I minded the applause. I stood up and took a quick bow for them. Mr. W. smiled and complimented me on my "showmanship." That's yet another cool thing about music: If you show off in sports, you're a "hotdog," if you show off in class, you're a "brainiac," but if you show off in drumming, people love it.

Mr. W. told me that my Latin rhythm was sounding a little stiff, and put on a CD for me to listen to. It was this old jazz album by Dizzy Gillespie.

This should help you out. It's a cat named Dizzy.

Yes, he said "cat." Music teachers have their own lingo.

Dizzy Gillespie, the trumpet player, right? My grandfather once told me about him.

Yeah. This is called "Cubana Be, Cubana Bop."

When the tune came on, I couldn't believe it. There were probably about five drummers on the track, and they were going crazy! The conga drum player was especially wild, playing insane fill-ins all over the place. At the same time, the trumpets were blasting like a herd of elephants, with Dizzy's horn flying high above everything else. Then, just when it seemed there couldn't possibly be any way to get more energy into the music, everyone stopped playing except the conga guy, and a man's voice started chanting in what sounded like Spanish. The chant got faster and faster, the congas got louder and louder, a whole chorus of men came in, shouting "Cubana Be, Cubana Bop" over and over, and the horns all roared back to life. Then, with one last explosion from the conga player, the song was over.

Could you feel that, Pez?

Mr. W. is the conductor of the All-City High School Jazz Band, which is how I got in. He knew that the nickname "Peasant" bugged me, so one day he started calling me "Pez" for short, which was much better.

Could I feel it? Oh, my God! That was the coolest thing I've ever heard in my life.

Good. You have about seven months to get that conga part down.

What do you mean?

Well, I've decided that the spring concert is going to be all Latin music, and that song is going to be the finale. Would you like to play congas on it?

Of course I was dying to play that part, but Mr. W. is one of those rare teachers who can actually take a joke.

Oh, I don't know, Mr. W. I was really hoping to play cowbell on it. Or ... maybe ... I don't know ... the triangle?

Get out of here, kid! You're gonna miss your bus!

I triumphantly popped my second-to-last Tic Tac into my mouth and strolled out of the room, whistling "Cubana Be, Cubana Bop."

My temporary good cheer lasted until I got on the bus. Renee Albert caught my eye (well, OK, she always catches my eye) and spoke. *How's the brain injury?*

Which brought me back to reality really, really fast.

I kept going toward the back of the bus without saying anything to Renee and sat down next to Annette. I had planned to tell her all about "Cubana Be, Cubana Bop," but now my mind was back on Jeffy.

I heard that, Steven. It's really cool that you were confident enough to just ignore her.

Ignore her? I didn't ignore her — I'm just too stupid to think of a comeback. And now I have to go home and find out what happened with my brother and how long I'll be grounded for making breakfast.

What?

Long story. When Jeffy fell this morning, I was making him oatmeal. I had him up on the stool, and my mom thinks he shouldn't be on there unless somebody's, like, an inch and a half away. So if he needed stitches or something, even though I was being NICE by making him what he wanted while the 'rents were SLEEPING, I'm going to get blamed.

Well, your mom was right, in a way.

What do you mean?

He DID fall, right? So he wasn't safe on the stool.

Thanks, Annette. Thanks a lot. That's exactly what I needed to hear right now. You're a very inspiring person, you know that?

I was just trying to . . .

Trying to what? Show me the light so I can be saved from being such a horrible brother? So little angel Jeffy can be safe from my evil cooking schemes?

I didn't mean to make you . . .

Feel bad? Well, you did. I've been worrying about this all stupid day!

By this point, we were pulling up to my stop. I got up to storm off the bus but had to wait while Renee got her stuff together in the middle of the aisle. Plus, Renee took her time walking off, too, so I had to plod along behind her. It's hard to storm and shuffle at the same time, let me tell you.

When I got off the bus, I watched Renee walk — no, glide — away. Then I looked up at Annette as the bus started to move. Maybe it was the slanted fall sun glaring off the window, but it almost looked like she was crying.

Great.

I let myself into the house and found my mom standing in the foyer, like she had been waiting for me. When I might be in trouble, I usually try to speak first, before the 'rents start in on me. So I plunged right in. *Mom, I've been worried all day. Is Jeffrey okay?*

She said, in this strange, soft voice, *Steven, your brother is really sick.*

Did I? Was it because he . . . ?

The fall this morning had nothing to do with it.

Whew! I'm off the hook.

But he's . . . really . . . sick.

And this was the absolute worst thing about last October 7th, the one moment I'll never forgive myself for. When my mother began to tell me that my baby brother had leukemia, my first feeling was relief.

THE **FAT CAT SAT**

Here is the entry I wrote in my English journal on October 8th:

I remember when I was eight and my mom was about to give birth to Jeffrey, my grandfather gave me a big pep talk on the way to the hospital.

Well, Muscles (yes, he really DID call me that), this is your big day.

My big day? Why is it my big day, Grampa?

Come on, Steven, it's not every day you become a big brother. And you are going to be very, very important from now on.

This was startling news to me. *Very important? Why? I'm not a mom. I'm not even a dad. I'm not even nine yet. I still have baby teeth, even.*

You're going to be very important because you are going to be your new baby's protector.

Really?

Yes, you are. Your baby isn't going to know all the things you know or be strong like you are, or anything.

And you are going to be very important to this baby, because you're not the mommy or the daddy. You're the big brother, and the baby is going to love you and need you SO much.

And for about ten or fifteen minutes there in the car, I felt great. I remember thinking, "Wow! A protector. Not everybody gets to be a protector! I'm gonna be like Robin Hood. I might even get to wear a badge. . . ."

Then Grampa nosed his huge Chevy Impala into a parking space at the hospital. By the time we got upstairs to the maternity ward, and I saw the balloons, the flowers everywhere, and my three other grandparents crowded around an incubator crying and smiling like they'd just won the Powerball Lotto, I was having second thoughts about this whole "protector" gig.

Still, though, I have always protected Jeffrey. When he was three and fell on a stick in our driveway, I was the one who took him inside and got a Band-Aid and his boo-boo bunny. When his little best friend, Alex, tried to push him off of the swing set last year, I got in trouble for pulling Alex down and screaming in his face until my mom dragged me away. Even when Jeffrey had a big asthma attack and had to be hospitalized overnight when he was one, I stood right next to his bed and held his hand for what seemed like hours and hours until he fell asleep. Then in the middle of the night when he woke up scared, I crawled into his bed with him, and our parents found us that way in the morning.

I haven't always liked being the Protector, but I think I have taken the job pretty seriously overall.

So how come when I wasn't looking, Jeffy got cancer?

• • •

The journal topic that day, I later learned, was "Discuss your favorite character in *Huckleberry Finn*."

The thing I couldn't believe was how this cancer thing turned the whole planet upside down in one day. I mean, it turns out that Jeffrey had to have been sick for a while without us knowing it. When my mom got him to the emergency room and the nurse took his temperature, it was a little over a hundred.

The nurse asked him how he felt, and he told her that he knew he had a fever and that his "parts" had been hurting for a long time. Meanwhile, his nose just kept bleeding and bleeding. The regular E.R. doctor must have thought this looked a bit unusual, so he called in a pediatrician. My mom told us that night that she couldn't believe what the pediatrician told Jeffrey to do next: "Please walk over to the desk there and get me a tissue." My mom was thinking, "My child is BLEEDING PROFUSELY and you want HIM to get YOU a tissue?" But Jeffrey got right up and started walking toward the main desk of the E.R. My mom said she suddenly noticed that Jeffrey was limping. As she told us this, after Jeffrey was already upstairs in bed, she started to weep.

How did I not notice this? Why did I need a doctor to show me? How long has he been limping? How long has my baby been limping around with a fever while I was too busy grading papers and making dinner to even LOOK at my Jeffy?

My dad, who wasn't looking too composed

either, came over and put his arm around her. He didn't say anything, though, so I chimed in.

Mom, we were ALL too busy to notice. It's not just you. He even told me this morning that he was cold and his parts hurt, and I just thought he was Jeffrey being Jeffrey. I was bummed that he interrupted my practicing to ask for breakfast. My own brother . . . and all he wanted was some oatmeal.

Now I was getting, truthfully, a bit weepy myself. See what I mean about cancer turning everything upside down? This pity festival went on for at least another hour, with each of us pretty much just saying over and over that this was somehow our fault. Now, let's face it — I'm smart enough to know logically that Jeffrey didn't get sick because I stole change from his piggy bank when he was three and bought Tic Tacs for my whole class with it. But for some reason on that first horrible night, it seemed as though everything I ever did to Jeffrey had probably caused some horrible genetic damage.

And now there we were, confessing our sins.

Finally, I asked my parents what was going to happen next. They told me that my mom would be taking Jeffy to Philadelphia, an hour and a half away, first thing in the morning, for some medical tests.

So he might not even have cancer, right? If the experts are in Philly, these local doctors are probably wrong pretty often. And then tomorrow night, you'll come back, right? And you'll tell us it was a mistake?

My dad chimed in, *Anything's possible, son.*

But Mom wasn't in a mood for optimism. *We won't be coming back tomorrow night, Steven.*

What do you mean you won't be coming back tomorrow night? What about Jeffrey's school? If he misses two days of kindergarten in a row, he'll probably miss, like, a whole letter of the alphabet. And what if it's a vowel? Then he'll have this huge problem with reading. He'll read, "The fat cat sat," but he'll think it says, "The ft ct st."

Very funny, Steven.

And what about your work, Mom?

Both of my parents got really, really quiet all of a sudden, and I knew this was not a good sign.

Finally, my dad spoke. *Mom might not be working for a while.*

But what? But why? How did . . . ?

Steven, I had a long talk with my principal today. There's a pretty good chance I'll be taking some time off of work.

Wow, Mom, you were pretty busy today.

She looked away.

I guess because I was nervous, I started to recap the day's events out loud. *So OK, here's October 7th with the Alper family. Wake up as normal people. Younger son gets nosebleed. Older son goes to school. Dad goes to work. Younger son goes to emergency room. Younger son allegedly has cancer. Mom quits job. Mom and younger son get ready to skip town. Father and older son stand around like idiots and prepare to buy a huge supply of —* *what? TV dinners?*

Please calm down, Steven. We are all going to have a big adjustment to make.

Adjustment? ADJUSTMENT? Getting a new car is an adjustment. Switching math classes is an adjustment. Finding out your brother has leukemia — supposedly —

and that your mom is now unemployed and that they're running off to the city in the morning, leaving you and your father to starve to death alone, is not an adjustment.

Steven! This isn't about you. How do you think your brother feels right now?

Then we had another one of these new, despairing silences. Until I had to ask a question that somehow hadn't occurred to me. *Ummm . . . Mom? How much does Jeffy know?*

It turned out that Jeffrey knew he might be pretty sick — try cauterizing a kid's gushing nose with a heat gun without him figuring out that something is up — but didn't understand too much about the details. My mom hadn't wanted to worry him prematurely. When she told him that he would have to go with her to the big city in the morning to see another doctor, all he had asked was, "Will Steven come, too?"

This was the one piece of information that put me over the edge. I started crying, but when my mom started coming over to hug me, I ran upstairs for bed. If I had known that this would basically be the last time I'd have both parents paying attention to me at once, I probably would have taken the hug.

I could hear my parents talking for a long, long time before I fell asleep, but nobody came up to check on me. Jeffy groaned in his sleep once or twice in the next room but never woke up. I was alone. I counted the little glowing stars on my ceiling, revisited my argument with Annette, played drum beats on a huge imaginary drum set in my head, and then realized one last thing I hadn't thought about since I'd walked in the door after school.

And I muttered to myself in the darkness, *Guess what, Mom? I'm going to be the star of my spring concert.*

JEFFREY'S VACATION

In the morning, I was the first one up, as usual. I was really hungry, for some odd reason, and I was thinking that Jeffrey was going to have a hard day. So I decided to surprise him with the oatmeal he had never gotten the day before. I got everything all cooked up and had just covered the pot when I heard little footsteps behind me.

I started to speak and turn at the same time, *Good morning, Jeffy. I made you some . . .*

Now, I knew Jeffrey was bruised up from his fall, and I also knew that bruises always look worse on the second day. But at that stage of the game, I didn't know how much worse bruises look on a kid with leukemia. When I turned around, I gasped and my hand came up to my mouth. Jeffrey had the two worst black eyes I'd ever seen, and his nose was swollen to about twice its normal size. He saw my reaction and winced.

What's wrong, Steven?

How does your face feel, Jeffy?

It feels thick.

Thick?

And hot. Why?

It's, ummm, a little swollen.

What do you mean? Do I look funny? What if the new doctor thinks I look stupid? I'm going to go look in the mirror.

Before I could even think of stopping him, he ran to the foyer and looked in our hallway mirror. I ran over, and he looked at me with horror in his eyes.

Steven, I look like a raccoon.

You do NOT look like a raccoon.

Actually, he looked like some deranged anteater, but I didn't figure that would be the thing to tell him.

Yes, I do. Oh, no. What if I stay this way forever?

You're not going to stay that way forever, Jeffy. People get black eyes all the time. If they never got better, the streets would be crowded with raccoon people. Soon, the raccoon people would find each other and breed.

I was on a roll here.

The preschools would fill up with strange ring-eyed children. Soon the raccoons would be taking over our streets, stealing from our garbage cans, leaving eerie trails of Dinty Moore beef stew cans in their wake. Gangs of them would haunt the malls, buying up all the black-and-gray-striped sportswear. THE RIVERS WOULD RISE! THE VALLEYS WOULD RUN WITH . . .

Steven, you're joking, right? What's for breakfast?

Oatmeal.

Yay! Moatmeal!

And just like that, Jeffrey was over his crisis. Which is pretty amazing. If I have a single zit, I want to crawl under my bed and hide with three days' worth of food. This kid looks like he just lost a box-ing match with a gorilla, and it takes him, like, five minutes and a bowl of hot cereal to forget about it.

While Jeffrey was eating, I snuck upstairs to warn the 'rents about Jeffrey's looks. I figured my mom was going to have enough shocks to deal with, so I should spare her this one if I could. It worked, or at least the 'rents managed to hide their reactions from Jeffrey when they came downstairs. We all sat at the break-fast table, pretending to be normal and cheerful. But you know how when you watch the Brady Bunch, you think, "Oh, come on! Nobody is this happy. What's wrong with you people? And who picks out your CLOTHES?" Well, breakfast was sort of like that, only instead of the clothing problem, we had an unmentionable cancer problem.

The good-byes were pretty uneventful, and Jeffrey even managed to bug me, which was probably a good sign.

On his way out the door, he turned to make fun of his brother. *You're going to schoo . . . oooo . . . . . llll. You're going to schhhooo . . . ooooo . . . llllll.*

If he had known what was coming up for his day, he would have been begging me to smuggle him to school in my backpack.

Once my mom and Jeffy left, my dad and I just kind of slid around the house, getting ready to face the day, not quite ready to face each other. We got into the car without word one being spoken, and on the actual ride, it was so quiet between us that I imagined I could hear the tire treads rubbing against the road. I couldn't wait to hop out of there and get into school, but somehow when we did pull up to the building, I didn't make any move to get out. My dad nearly looked at me, and I kind of stared through his right shoulder. After about a minute of this, we both mumbled at once, *Well . . . OK . . .*

That was the deepest conversation we would have all week. I got out and went to school. When I came around the corner toward homeroom, I saw Renee and forgot about everything else. She was wearing this shirt that was clingy and shiny and maybe a little bit see-through, with a skirt that just wasn't quite doing its whole job. I stopped and stared for far too long, until Annette banged my arm.

Check HER out. There's no way that doesn't violate the dress code! I hope she gets marched to the office. It's disgusting! Don't you think so, Steven? Steven? Ssstteeee . . . vvvveeeeennnnn?

So at least Annette was talking to me again. When I tore my eyes away from Renee, the contrast was pretty strong.

Annette was doing the 1970s retro thing, I guess. She had on this sweater that was pretty tough to describe. It looked like what you'd get if all of your parents' favorite dinosaur-rock bands died and left you all their extra fabric, and then a little old blind lady sewed all the pieces together with a tasteful burnt-orange thread. It made a statement, though. It truly did.

Uuhhhh, yeah. Sure.

Oh my God, I almost forgot! Steven, how's your brother? Did you get in trouble?

I didn't get in trouble. And he's . . . fine. I'm sorry I yelled at you on the bus.

I'm sorry, too, Steven. I know how much you care about your brother, and you must have been worried.

Me, worried? Maybe. You might notice that this would have been the perfect time to tell Annette the whole story, but for some reason I didn't want anyone at school to know. It turned out that once I decided not to tell Annette at that moment, it became almost impossible to tell anybody. So for the rest of the week, while I was walking around in a fog, I didn't say a word. I joked around with my friends, played the drums, sat in classes, and acted even more lame than usual around Renee, but I didn't let anybody know what was going on with Jeffrey.

It was weird. The longer I pretended everything was normal at school, the more I believed everything was normal. I started thinking over and over again, "Doctors are wrong all the time. You hear about these malpractice things every day where people get medicine that's not even theirs. I bet Jeffy's down there in Philly, guzzling cheesesteaks, having a great time, getting waited on hand and foot by Mom, while I'm up here eating all the Hungry Man dinners on the East Coast, and Dad is pretending I'm some odd thirteen-year-old stranger who's just moved in to keep the microwave warm while his REAL family is away."

Meanwhile, that wasn't quite the way things were actually happening. I found out later that my dad was getting horrible phone reports from my mom for an hour each night, long after Jeffy and I were both asleep. So, in a sense, my dad was shielding me by not talking. I could have used some companionship that week, but maybe I wouldn't have believed any-thing about Jeffy until I was ready, no matter what Dad said.

The week went by in this half-awake sort of way, for me at least. While I was staring at Renee in fifth-period math and praying nobody would make her change her outfit, Jeffrey was getting strapped down to a gurney. While Annette was smacking my arm yet again, a doctor was shoving a huge needle through Jeffrey's back into his hip, all the way into the bone. While I was laughing at some joke the teacher hadn't heard, Jeffrey was screaming as the needle sucked the bone marrow out of him. But I was just thinking about me and about how ridiculous it was that everyone except me was getting so freaked out over a stupid bloody nose.

The only times all week when I truly felt all right were the times when I was playing the drums. I have always been pretty serious about hitting the old practice pad at home, but now that I was living in the Conversation-Free TV-Dinner Zombie Zone, I basically had nothing else to do. It was truly ridiculous — within days after Jeffrey's fall, I got to the point where I was spending twenty-five minutes a night playing double-stroke rolls on the surface of a dime without missing or even moving the coin. I knew my drum teacher, Mr. Stoll, was going to be pretty impressed with my progress. Before this, he had assigned me maybe two pages in each of three different exercise books every week. But now I was doing two pages per NIGHT in each book. I was also practicing for my upcoming conga drum stardom. Mr. Watras lent me a pair of really expensive bongos to use at home, along with a huge stack of ancient Latin jazz records. He had even called Mr. Stoll (they had played in bands together — isn't it weird when grown-ups have actual lives?) to tell him what I should practice on them. Fortunately, my dad has a Stone Age stereo system in the basement with an actual turntable, so I was playing along with at least one whole Latin record each night.

I know, I know, you're probably thinking that my new superhuman drum schedule must have been cutting into my homework time. And in fact you would be correct, except that I completely stopped doing homework the day Jeffrey got sick and didn't start again until I got busted by my teachers much, much later. I sometimes looked at my homework assignments and occasionally even wrote a heading on a piece of paper as if I was about to attempt the work, but somehow I wound up going to school empty-handed day after day. In class, too, I just started basically blanking out every period, every day.

You might also think that lots of my friends would notice it if their pal Steven stopped doing schoolwork, started staring off into space 85% of the time, and suddenly avoided any mention of his family. But you'd be wrong there. I think every group of friends has a "guy" for each different function — like the "sympathetic guy," the "funny guy," the "jock," the "guy who gets picked on." I had never really thought about it before, but apparently to my friends I had two roles: "funny guy" and "drum guy." So as long as I carried a pair of sticks and kept the humor coming, nobody was going to guess anything was up with me.

Except Annette. Pretty much every morning in

homeroom, she would ask me what was wrong. The first few days, I would make a joke or say that nothing was the matter. After that, I got more and more impatient with her every time she asked. I kept hoping that if I was just snappish enough, she would leave me alone. Meanwhile, she stuck with me. She was my best friend — maybe my only true friend — but I wasn't seeing it.

There was only one way I was communicating with the outside world at all, and that was my English journal. Miss Palma has this rule that if you fold down your page, it shows your journal is private. Well, my journal was starting to look like some kind of weird origami factory, with page after page folded on different angles and edges sticking out all over the place. Of course, Miss Palma had to know that I was doing something strange, because again and again I'd be writing three and four pages, supposedly about these completely impersonal topics, and then folding down all the pages one by one. But either she really believed I was having deep emotional reactions to questions like, "Should our school have uniforms?" or she was just giving me enough rope to hang myself.

Here's the journal I wrote on the sixth day after my mom and Jeffrey went away, the day before they came back:

If I could say anything I wanted to, to anyone in the world, right now, I would be all over Annette.

Who died and left you Sherlock Holmes? Why is it your business if I don't do my math homework? AND even if that somehow, in some way that only you can understand, is your business, how is it your business WHY I didn't do it? First of all, you're not my mother, and second, even if you were my mother, you wouldn't care. You'd be in Philadelphia, buying soft pretzels and Italian ices for your baby son, not checking in with your microwave-oven maintenance son. Second of all, this is a free country. I have a God-given, American right to avoid homework if that helps me in the pursuit of happiness. Don't you pay ANY attention in social studies? I swear to God, Annette,

I haven't even read the chapter for this week yet, but I know more than you do. You should move to Cuba. Immediately.

And don't get me started on my father, Mister Personality. If you ask me, he could use a good, stern talking-to as well.

Dad, how about sometime this week, just for kicks, you try making eye contact with me? Would that be so painful? And how about you ask how my day was — and then actually listen while I'm telling you? Here are some sample questions you can try until you get good at this: Son, what did you learn in school today? How's the drumming going? Are you at all worried that your mother and brother have disappeared into thin air and nobody's telling you Thing One about what's going on with them? How about them Yankees? I think they might win the Series this year! Any supposed father who doesn't even address his son say, once a day, isn't even a father, in my opinion. So thanks for being my sperm donor, Pop.

Ooohhh, and then there's my egg donor. Why hasn't she checked in with me this week? Am I so drastically unimportant? Is Philadelphia such a remote region of the planet that her cell phone won't work? Also, has she not noticed that there are these things called "pay phones" that one can use for long-distance communication when all else fails? Jeez, she could have sent a pigeon with a message banded to its leg and it would have gotten to me by now. Bang on a log, send me a smoke signal, SOMETHING!

Finally, there's Mr. Raccoon Face himself — Jeffrey. I'm sure that by now his face is looking better, whatever little virus he had that gave him the fever is gone, and he's thoroughly enjoying his steady diet of high-fat, high-sugar street-vendor food that he doesn't even have to microwave for himself. Unlike his heroic older brother, who is gradually dying of freezer-burned-food poisoning. By now, he probably has every single nurse there wrapped around his finger, waiting on him hand and foot, rushing over to get him the remote control for his 300-channel satellite TV so he doesn't have to exert himself. Plus, all the nurses probably look like older, even better-developed versions of Renee Albert. And they're scurrying about, fluffing Jeffrey's pillows, while I'm stuck here, getting lectured daily by Annette, just because I'm skipping an assignment here and there while the rest of my family is ON VACATION!

• • •

You can see how folding the pages down was a good call on my part.

The climax of the week actually came that afternoon. It was an All-City jazz band rehearsal day, and when I got to the high school, I found out that Brian was at home sick. Because of that, I got to play the drum set for an hour and forty minutes straight. I was smokin', too. I always play well when I start out in a bad mood, for some reason, plus I had been practicing so much that my wrists were just superquick. We played through some of our usual repertoire, like the theme from this old 1970s TV show called *Barney Miller,* some old jazz standards from the 1940s, and a Disney medley, which was actually far, far cooler than it sounds. Then we got into one of the new Latin pieces, a Dizzy Gillespie song called "Manteca." Without two drummers, I had to play crazy fast to make the percussion parts sound full enough. My right foot was pounding out accents, my left foot was clicking the hi-hat cymbals on beats "two" and "four," my right hand was going back and forth between the cowbell and a crash cymbal, and my left hand was flying from the snare drum to the tom-toms and back. Suddenly, a rare and amazing thing happened to me: I was in the Zone. You know how baseball players sometimes talk about games when the ball seemed to be coming at their bats in slow motion, looking like a gigantic freeze-frame cantaloupe just waiting to be pounded? That's how this felt, like I could do no wrong. I was so far up inside the beat that I wasn't thinking at all — my body just did everything, perfectly, almost by itself. Mr. Watras, who usually grades papers while a student conducts us through practice, stopped what he was doing to watch me. I could see a huge grin on his face, but I wasn't affected too much by that until I remembered it later — I was just grooving on drummer autopilot.

Then Renee walked in to visit her boyfriend,

Biff the Guitar Wonder. She must have come straight from varsity cheering practice — she was one of only three eighth graders who got to practice with the high school squad — because she was wearing her uniform. I hope to God she had been watching for a while before I noticed her, because as soon as I looked up, the shock of seeing her there, wearing only small amounts of Lycra and spandex, and looking right at me, knocked me out of the Zone. Far out of the Zone. As in, "Oooohhh, Pez, you dropped a stick — right in the middle of a song! And it went tumbling across the room at about 90 miles an hour! And it smashed into the bell of some senior's trumpet! And who knew brass was so flimsy, anyway?"

By the way, the sound of a high school jazz band falling apart in mid-tune, while one of the trumpet players is screaming at the drummer at the top of his lungs and the piano player is in the throes of a mad laughing fit, is just not something you want to hear. And it's certainly not something you want the hottest girl in eighth grade to hear. Renee looked away, but there was definitely a hint of a pleased smirk on her face for a split second. Then I was distracted by the senior trumpeter's raging, top-volume, spit-spewing barrage of verbal abuse in my face. By the time Mr. Watras had stopped this guy from busting me open like an overstuffed piñata, Renee was gone, I was mortified, and Annette was still kind of snorting and giggling. Which made for a fun ride home, although at least she couldn't snicker uncontrollably and bug me about my homework record at the same time.

The next morning, my mom and Jeffrey returned from Philadelphia.

NO MORE VACATION

If you're like me, you wake up on a nice Saturday morning in the autumn, and you want to smell the crisp fall air, sit halfway up, stretch, and then go back to sleep until about noon. But if you're like me on this particular Saturday morning, you also want to wake up so you can see your mom and brother when they get home.

Somehow, at least half of me believed that my mom and Jeffrey would come hopping out of the car, run into the house, and share a good laugh with my dad and me about the little false alarm they had been through. You know, like, "Ha-ha. Those silly doctors. Can you be-LIEVE they mistook a nosebleed for leukemia? It's just so ridiculous!" And then I'd pout for a while about how my mom hadn't called me all week and tease Jeffrey about how chubby he was getting from all the cheesesteaks and soft pretzels down in Philly, and then go back to sleep for a nice lazy Saturday nap.

When my mom finally pulled into our driveway,

64

though, I saw that Jeffrey was asleep in the backseat, and I started to get nervous. Jeffrey never, ever used to sleep on car rides. I am a big car-ride sleeper, maybe the biggest. But Jeffrey was usually just blabbing away for hours on end on any kind of road trip. Once we drove to the Outer Banks for a vacation when Jeffrey was three, and he stayed up until after midnight on the way down. At about 10 p.m., while he was giving me a lecture on the various Rescue Heroes, and why a Voice-Tech Rescue Hero is completely different from a Body Force Rescue Hero, my parents pulled off the highway into a Cracker Barrel restaurant and rented a *Charlotte's Web* book on tape to shut him up. But even then, he made my mom stop the tape every fifteen minutes so he could ask long strings of questions. Have you ever tried to sleep while a pint-size maniac is rattling off hundreds of detailed inquiries about the web-spinning mechanisms of the common barn spider? Granted, it was strangely amusing to watch the accountant and the English teacher attempt to explain arachnid biology, but overall, I was about ready to strap myself to the

roof rack by the time Jeffrey finally nodded off —
just in time for us to arrive at our rental house, so he
could wake up again and ask a million new questions
about the locale, the sleeping arrangements, which
pajamas he should wear, and why Steven always gets
to sleep on the couch when all HE gets is a stupid bed.

Anyway, that's why a sleeping Jeffrey didn't strike
me as a reassuring sign. My mom left him in the car
and walked up to the door to hug us. When she took
off her sunglasses, I couldn't believe how old and
tired she looked. After my hug, she stepped back for
a moment, and I made a pretty major social blunder.

*So, Mom, everything's OK, right? This whole cancer
mistake is all sorted out?*

She looked at me like I had just asked her for a
cigarette. *Steven, this is no time to joke. Your brother is a
very, very sick boy.*

He is? I just figured it was all a big mistake.

Mistake? MISTAKE?

*Well, you know, when you didn't call and all, I
assumed that . . .*

What do you mean, when I didn't call? You know I spoke to your father every single night.

Well, no, actually Dad never . . .

YOU DIDN'T TELL HIM THAT I CALLED? Didn't you tell him anything? He at least knows about Jeffrey's condition, doesn't he?

Honey, I . . . ummm . . .

Oh, boy. There was something going on here, for sure. But I wouldn't find out much about it right then, because Jeffrey woke up right at that instant and knocked on the car window. My mom immediately jogged back out to him. My dad gave me a sheepish look and started off slowly after her. I could tell by the slouchy way he was walking that he didn't exactly relish the thought of arriving at the car and facing his angry wife and sick son, but on the other hand, he certainly couldn't just stay in the doorway because then he'd have to face me.

I stayed inside while my dad made a big show of grabbing the bags from the trunk and my mom carried Jeffrey in. Jeffrey looked really beat, too, although his black eyes had faded to yellow and his nose had gone back to normal. I was afraid of what I would say to him, but as usual, I was worried about the wrong thing. I should have been afraid of what he would say to me. He started right in, and although his voice was kind of gravelly, the words came out at lightning speed.

Steven, Steven! You should have seen it! The hospital was HUGE! And I had a real BED! And you could MOVE it! The head sat UP, and the FEET did, too! And the doctors came and put a needle in my BACK! And then I couldn't move for an HOUR! But Mommy got me a cool book about KNIGHTS IN SHINING ARMOR. She sat on the floor and read it to me upside down so I wouldn't be BORED! But I was anyway. And they gave me sleepy medicine and put a special TUBE in my chest called a catheter. And another time they put a needle all the way in my HIPBONE. It HURT! Then they took out some inside bone stuff called BONE NARROW. And my BONE NARROW is sick. So they put another needle in my back yesterday with the THROW-UP MEDICINE! And I had a needle stuck in my chest for FIVE DAYS!

He paused to look at my mom for confirmation. *FIVE days, right, Mommy?*

When he pushed up off of her shoulder to look at her, I looked, too. I couldn't believe it — she was crying silently. Her voice came out all trembly when she said, *Yes, baby. Five days.*

I was standing there with my head reeling. My brother was really sick, so sick that they had to stick a needle in him to take out the marrow from his bones. He was so sick that they had to stab a needle into his spinal cord. He was so sick that my dad couldn't bear to tell me about it and that my mom was instantly crying as soon as the details were mentioned.

And everything I had been thinking all week was 100% wrong.

My mom recovered enough to ask Jeffrey if he wanted a snack, but he turned kind of green and said he wasn't hungry. I found out later that he had begun chemotherapy for his disease, and that one of the many side effects was nausea.

Can you put me down? Can I hug Daddy?

Of course, honey.

Daddy! I missed you!

Despite my shock, I remember thinking, "Well, you didn't miss much this week, Dad-wise."

And I missed you, Steven. I thought you might be lonely without me, so I got you a souvenir.

At this, Jeffrey pulled something out of his pocket. It was a box of orange Tic Tacs. I couldn't believe it — in the middle of this horrible experience, Jeffrey had thought of me and had even managed to find me a box of my favorite candy. I thanked him, and I really meant it, which wasn't always the case when I showed gratitude to Jeffrey. I remember when he was maybe a year old, Jeffrey went through a phase of picking up random objects from the floor and giving them to one of us — usually me. I'd be right in the middle of building a gigantic Lego space station or whatever, and he would come toddling over and present me with that month's copy of *Better Homes and Gardens* or the TV remote or a used tissue. And my mom would make me stop what I was doing and say thank you. I hated it at the time, and my annoyance had blinded me to just how generous my little brother really was.

OK, before this turns into some kind of weepy lovefest, I will tell you what happened next. I took out the Tic Tacs, popped one into my mouth, and offered one to Jeffrey. He held out his hand, pinched the Tic Tac between his thumb and pointer finger, flipped it into his mouth — and promptly threw up onto my sneakers.

My first reaction was to shout, *Jeffrey! Mom!*

Jeffrey looked up at me with the hurt-little-deer eyes he gets when I yell at him and ran to the bathroom. Mom told me not to move, got a white plastic kitchen garbage bag, made me step onto it, and then took my sneakers off of me as I stepped off of the bag. My dad was just kind of staring at everything with a baffled expression, until my mother told him to go after Jeffrey. Then she turned back to me and told me to stay still — even though I was dying to take off my favorite sweatpants, which now had gore-spattered cuffs. She was dialing her cell phone at top speed, which I couldn't figure out until she started talking into it.

Hello. This is Mrs. Alper, Jeffrey Alper's mother. He's a patient in Clinical Trial Number 366. They told me to call if he . . . OK, I'll hold.

Mom, what's going on? Why do you have to call . . .

Is this the nurse? OK, Jeffrey left there two hours ago, and he just vomited. What should we do?

I was thinking a quicker cleanup might be a great place to start, but nobody was asking me for guidance here. In fact, my mom was leaning way down by the garbage bag, examining the vomit, and any interruption of this bizarre task seemed unwise.

No, there's no blood in it. Well, my older son gave him a Tic Tac. Orange. Do we have to adjust his meds? Yes? And you'll fax the adjustments to Doctor Purow here? I should call him in about . . . an hour? OK, thanks. She hung up and turned to me. *Steven, we have to be really careful with what Jeffrey eats for a while.*

As I took off my sweats and my mom started in on my sneakers with some paper towels and a can of carpet cleaner, I muttered, *Now you tell me.*

My mom stopped, looked up at me, laughed a little, and surprised me with a quick hug. *I missed you, Steven.*

I missed you, too, Mom.

Now go tell your brother you're not mad at him, OK?

And I realized I actually wasn't mad at him. All in all, this had been quite the morning for surprises. I went into the bathroom, threw my socks in the hamper — they looked clean, but just in case — and put my arms around Jeffrey. My dad was there, sitting on the closed toilet seat, trying to be comforting, but he really hadn't gotten his bearings yet with this cancer situation. I think he was relieved when Jeffrey leaned right into me. I started my old, trusty "Hush, Jeffy" chant, my dad tiptoed out, and after a while Jeffrey calmed down.

I looked right into his huge blue eyes and said, *Jeffy, it's OK. I'm not mad at you for throwing up on my shoes. Can you do me a favor next time, though?*

What?

Please aim for my dress shoes. I hate 'em!

Hee-hee-hee . . . 'K, Steven.

Now let's brush the taste out of your mouth and go ... I don't know ... ummm ... how about a drum lesson?

Yay! Drum lesson!

We went down to the basement. Jeffrey banged around on my drum set for twenty minutes or so and things felt normal again, for a little while. Then Jeffrey told me he wanted to take a nap, which he hadn't done for at least six months. I figured he was probably tired after the week he'd had, so I took him up. Mom and Dad were clearly having a very intense discussion in the dining room, so we just went right past them to his room. He wanted to wear his PJs, so I got them out for him. He took off his shirt and pants, which left him standing there in his *Star Wars: Episode I* underwear. As I handed over the pajamas, I saw that his lower back had a fairly massive bruise on it from the bone-marrow aspiration (although I didn't know the name of the procedure yet). When he put the shirt over his head, I got a quick glimpse of bruising along his spine, too. I didn't say anything about the bruises, though. I read him two chapters of

The Trumpet of the Swan, tucked him in with his stuffed-animal pet dog — cleverly named Dog-Dog, by the way — and walked downstairs to the dining room.

I was somewhat sure I wanted to know what was going on with my little brother.

When I walked into the room, my parents were both clearly agitated. They both jumped in at once, my mom trying to tell me how she had called every night, my dad trying to explain why he hadn't told me. I shocked myself by telling them I didn't care about any of that, that they should just give me the medical report on Jeffrey.

So they did.

Jeffrey had been diagnosed with ALL, which stands for acute lymphoblastic leukemia, a form of blood cancer in which certain types of white blood cells become deformed and multiply rapidly. Because the deformed cells, which are called blasts, don't do the jobs they are supposed to do and because they compete with the good kinds of blood cells for survival, the disease is 100% fatal if it isn't treated.

The reason why his nosebleed had been so bad is that the leukemia had drastically reduced the number of platelets in Jeffrey's blood so that it wasn't clotting normally. That was also why he was bruising so easily. When he had first arrived in Philly, the doctors had run a huge battery of tests to determine how bad Jeffrey's cancer was, whether it had spread to other systems in his body, and how likely he was to recover. Things weren't as ugly as they could have been — the cancer hadn't gone to other systems — but they weren't great, either. My baby brother had what they considered a "moderate-risk" case. That meant his odds of surviving this were over 50%, but not by much.

Which meant his chances of dying were *under* 50% but, again, not by much.

No wonder my mom was weepy and my dad was a zombie.

We talked a little more, about things like scheduling — my mom and Jeffrey would be in Philadelphia at least two days a week for the first month of treatment — and how to handle telling people. It turned out that my mom's parents already knew and so did a lot of extended family members. The reason nobody had called the house about it yet was that my mom had asked that nobody call or visit until she and Jeffrey were home. My mom's principal knew and so did some of her closest friends, but most of her school didn't know. I didn't know what my dad had said or not said at work, but from his general level of communication that week, I had a feeling he had been clammed up pretty tight with everyone. On the other hand, his coworkers would have had to be blind and deaf not to have noticed the sudden changes in what was now passing for his personality.

Jeffrey's school would have to know, of course.

My mom had another thought, too. *And what about your school, Steven? Would you like me to call your school counselor? We could have a conference call with your teachers.*

Or you could just shoot me now and get it over with.

Steven! It makes perfect sense to alert the school staff to a situation where one of the students might need additional support.

What additional support? A group hug in homeroom every morning? Maybe my teachers could write you little notes in my agenda book. Or how about you sign me up for a nice counseling group? Perhaps you could make me look like more of a dork to my peers. Do you think you could get me a seat on the short bus?

WHAT has gotten into you, Steven? I'm trying to help you here. The doctors told me that siblings of (she kind of had to swallow before she could get this next part out) *cancer patients find the experience very stressful and . . .*

Stressful? STRESSFUL? Why should this be stressful? Just because my mom and brother disappear for a week and nobody tells me anything, and then they come back, and my brother is barfing right and left, with bruises all over him? And he can't even stay awake, and his little back is all . . . all . . .

Then I busted out crying, which I'm sure was a great comfort to everyone. At least, it shut me up for a while. My mom put her arms around me, and we stayed like that so long that my neck was getting a crick in it. Now, normally I am not the biggest fan of being hugged by my mother in broad daylight at this point in my adolescent years, but I must say, it felt pretty nice right then.

When I finally pulled away a bit, I looked at my mom and pleaded, *Please don't call my school. I'm fine.*

(Yeah, teenage boys who are fine always cry on their mothers' shoulders until they leave a snot trail.)

Okay, Steven — for now, we won't call.

So they didn't call, and if any of my mom's friends told their kids, it didn't get back to me for those first few weeks. As for me, I was always the perfect big brother for Jeffrey, the silent microwave-oven mate that my dad seemed to want, and completely sarcastic and horrible to my mom. Don't ask me why I dumped everything on her, but I did. Meanwhile, at school, I still kept plowing along, practicing drums, writing journals, completely bagging all of my homework assignments, and faking human interaction with the people around me.

Inside my head, though, I had a whole new activity: bargaining.

TAKE ME!

Once I was forced to believe that Jeffrey really had cancer, my mind played another big trick on me. I started to think that if I just made the right promises to God, he would magically make Jeffrey all better again. And the promises just popped into my head, right and left, day and night. This made for a tough couple of weeks.

I'd be in the lunch line at school, and a pack of Ring Dings would catch my eye. I'd say to myself, "OK, if I don't eat those, Jeffrey will get better." Or I'd promise things like, "If I never hit Jeffrey again, he'll get better." About twenty times a day, too, I'd swear that I'd never think impure thoughts about Renee Albert again if Jeffrey would be all right. But let's face it — I am a thirteen-year-old American male. I have no willpower. So every night I'd go to bed totally convinced that I was going to gain twenty pounds and be a fat, violent pervert forever and that my little brother was doomed.

Then in the morning, I'd start all over, like, "I'll floss every single day, even between the molars, if . . ."

Of course, there were times when I wasn't bargaining, but those were generally just times when I was busy BREAKING the promises. It was like the exact opposite of Lent; I would swear to give things up and then immediately do them. I was a mess.

When I realized how bad I was at giving things up, I tried to find other deals I could make with God. One day in gym, we were hitting softballs with this pitching machine that the baseball team uses for training — which we almost never get to use, but it was a really nice day and the teachers must have been desperate to get outside one last time before winter started. So I was telling myself, "All righty, if I hit this next pitch, Jeffrey is OK." Then I'd miss, because with my thick glasses, I basically have no depth perception at all. So immediately I'd be at it again, "OK . . . how 'bout two out of three?" Strike two! "Four for six?" Whiff! "Seven out of ten?" Naturally, I know what a spazmo I am at sports (yeah, I know drummers are supposed to be coordinated, but it doesn't matter how coordinated you are if you're as blind as a bat), so I know I should have found some smarter bets to make.

And I did. By the end of the first week, I was scrounging at the bottom of the barrel for deals to make. Here's a pathetic one: "Here goes a good offer, Lord. If that bird on that tree over there flies away within ten seconds, Jeffrey is cured." That was in the middle of math class, while I was staring out the window as the class checked the homework I hadn't done. Unfortunately, I got distracted by the teacher's despairing cry.

Alper, any chance you can answer number 37?

When I looked back out there, the bird was long gone, probably scared off by the outburst of yelling that was going on in my classroom. I was fairly certain it had been longer than ten seconds between when I first looked away and the moment when the teacher's attempt to engage me devolved into top-volume, random threats to my safety, but we'll never know for sure.

As usual, drumming was my big escape from all

this reality stuff. Rehearsals and practice times by myself were like these little islands of "OK" in a vast sea of "Holy crap!" So I hopped from little musical island to little musical island. One day, a weird thing happened to me. I left math class to go to the bathroom, and on my way back, I heard this beautiful piano-playing coming from the band room. Now, of course, I knew it had to be Annette — she was the only unbelievable keyboard prodigy in the building, and I knew that she had this independent-study piano period. But when I walked over and stuck my head in the band room door, I couldn't really process what I was seeing. There was this truly pretty girl sitting at the piano, with this amazing posture and her hair falling long around her face in a quite non-Annette-ish way and a serene look I had never noticed on her face before. She finished the piece and looked up after a long, long time — I would be toasted like a barbecue wiener when I got back to math — and blushed. She actually BLUSHED. It was like, as soon as the music disappeared, so did "Smooth Annette."

Then she mumbled, *Chopin.*

What?

That piece. It's Chopin. I'm getting ready for an audition at Juilliard next month, but I'm not nearly ready yet.

You're kidding, right? That was . . . uhhh . . . the best thing I've ever seen, ever. Ever. What's at Juilliard?

It's a famous music school in Manhattan. They have an intensive program for high school students, every Saturday from 8:00 to 1:00.

So you'd have to get up around 6:00 to get there?

I'd have to get up around 4:30 to get there, but my parents are willing to drive me, and . . .

Don't you want to have some free time on Saturdays?

Steven, this is . . . oh, forget it. Wanna try something?

Suddenly, another new Annette had sprung up. She had kind of a mischievous, flirty grin on her face.

Sure.

Sit down at the drum set. Go ahead. Now get ready to play what you hear, OK?

Ummm . . . all right.

And she burst into this fantastic, complicated

jazz thing. So I tried to play along with the ding ding-a-ding ride cymbal thing that always works for jazz and immediately got the beat all turned around and messed up. Annette stopped playing and laughed. She looked at me and jumped in again. Again, I got ruined in seconds. So she jumped in for another go-around. And another. And another.

Finally, I had to ask, *What . . . is . . . this?*

Oh, it's just a little something I picked up off a CD this week. It's called "Take Five." It's by this piano player named Dave Brubeck, from, like, 1963.

Why can't I play it?

Well, the beat is in five-four instead of four-four.

Huh?

You have to count five beats in every measure instead of four. That's why it's called "Take Five." Wanna take another shot?

Just then the bell rang, and I realized I had now officially skipped out of my first class ever. Annette just smiled that new smile again and flipped me a CD-R disc.

Here it is. Learn it!

Then she bopped off down the hall with the old bunny-on-puppet-strings walk I was used to, leaving me to wonder what had just happened. I was fairly sure that SOMETHING had.

Things were happening at home, too. Around the second week of Jeffrey's treatment, I guess word got out among my parents' friends that it was time to acknowledge Jeffrey's illness. All of a sudden, as if somebody had thrown a switch, phone calls started pouring in. Cards jammed up our mailbox. A flood of concerned grown-ups started pulling up to our house with baskets and bags of food, flowers, balloons, toys. I admit that the edible stuff gave me a nice break from being the microwave Hot Pockets poster child, but the whole scene was kind of bizarre. You can picture it: The well-wisher comes in. We all thank him or (more often) her as the Tupperware is handed over. Then everybody stands around awkwardly while the visitor tries to find appropriate things to say to my parents. If I'm around, it's weird — they ask me how I am, but I can't actually tell them about anything that's going on in 90% of my life — they really mean, "How are you, specifically with regard to your brother's health crisis?" And if Jeffrey is there, it's the biggest nightmare of all. Half of them try to be cheery, no matter what. So they act all loud and hearty, swinging Jeffrey around and telling corny jokes. Meanwhile, I'm standing there, mentally shouting at them, "Be gentle, you moron! DON'T BRUISE HIM! Please . . . step . . . away . . . from . . . the . . . boy." The other half are solemn, no matter what, which is equally horrendous. Because Jeffrey is such a naturally happy kid, he wasn't generally downhearted in those early days, despite the illness. Sometimes, he had really bad aches, especially in his legs, and he was tired a lot of the time, and the chemotherapy drugs were making him feel pretty rotten physically. But mentally, he was Jeffrey — the kid wanted to laugh and play and maybe watch Nickelodeon when things got too exhausting. And when the "frowny people" came, they almost *wanted* to see Jeff be a sad, sick boy — to EARN the pot roast they were carrying, or whatever. And those visits dampened his spirits, for a while at least.

After a week or so, though, Jeffrey and I made a game of it. As somebody started up our front walk, carrying the obligatory gigantic shopping bag, I would say, *OK, Jeff, what do you think — frowny or cheery?*

Definitely cheery, I think. We've had three frownies in a row.

You may be right, little man. We are due for a cheery, right about now. But she's looking a bit nervous; I'll bet you a buck she's gonna be a frowner.

Then we'd open the door, smirk at each other throughout the visit, and finally assign the visitor a score after she left. No matter how horrendous the experience had been, I could usually get Jeffrey to laugh by acting like a sports commentator.

A tremendous effort by kind, old Mrs. Jacobs from the accounts payable department. She brings an apple pie — but wait a minute. It's store-bought! That's a mandatory deduction, Jeff. We'll have to give her a five out of ten for baked goods. In the behavior category, she's definitely cheery — Jeff, I owe you a dollar, you gambling shark. But she clears her throat repeatedly, a clear sign of discomfort. On the other hand, she DID pat your head pretty vigorously. I'm going to have to call that a seven.

But she smelled kind of funny, Steven. Is that points off?

Ooohhh, it is! Another mandatory deduction. Was it a dirt smell or an oldness smell?

Oldness.

OK, that's another mandatory deduction — why don't we call this a six, overall?

Meanwhile, my parents would tell us to be nice if they saw all this, but I got the feeling it amused my dad as much as anything else had since Jeff's nosebleed.

Near the end of Jeffrey's first month of treatment, there was a big dance at school — the first one of my eighth-grade year, which is supposed to be some sort of big deal. You can imagine how much I felt like getting down and partying at that point, but of course I had to go. It was on a Friday night, one of the nights when Jeffrey was home, and he had been too weak to do anything but watch videos and throw up all day. For about half an hour before dinner, I tried to get him to play checkers, but he finally just wiped the pieces off the board and told me to go away.

I could believe a lot of things and had been forced to over the course of that month, but getting kicked out of a checker game by my baby brother was pretty tough to swallow. This was the kid who used to toddle over to my bed at 6 o'clock every weekend morning to pull on my blankets so I'd get up and watch cartoons with him. This was the kid who once made me play Hungry Hungry Hippos for an hour straight, until I thought my hands were going to fall off from slamming down those dumb little levers to make the hippos' heads move. This was the kid who had spent entire days at a time begging me to play Chutes and Ladders with him. And now he was feeling too sick to play with me.

And I know this is a selfish reaction, but my thought at the time was, "Oh, great. I'm not even at the dance yet, and I'm already getting rejected. What an ego boost!"

I was starting to get nervous about this dance.

I went through every possible clothing combination I own, but somehow none of my dozens of black rock-band T-shirts seemed to match with any of my three identical pairs of Old Navy jeans. And I was still standing in my room, with only my pants on, blasting WZZO, trying not to think about how horrendous Jeffrey must be feeling while I was running off to a dance, and randomly tossing shirts to and fro when my mom appeared in the doorway.

Honey, we have to hurry if you want to get to this dance. Since your father's at that big dinner meeting at work, I have to drive you and take Jeffrey with us. And I don't think your brother is going to be awake much longer.

I know, Mom. I just look like a dork-master in every shirt I own.

You do not look like a — what is it? — "dork-master," Steven. You look like a handsome young man . . . although you might want to zip your fly.

Mom!

What? Should I have not told you and left it for everyone else to notice at the dance?

MOM! Would you please let me get dressed?

We don't have time for one of your big insecurity scenes here, Steven. Let's see what you have in your closet.

She opened the closet doors and started thumbing through the clothes I had hanging there, giving little motherly comments.

This one looks great with your brown eyes. . . . This one makes you look nice and muscular. . . .

MOM!

This one is too formal. . . . This one is stained. WHY is a dirty shirt hanging in your closet? This one is PERFECT. Now put it on.

MOM! That one is purple. I haven't worn it ONCE since the day Grandma gave it to me. I'll look like Barney!

Oh, Steven. Barney is purple and GREEN. You will look nothing like him. Plus, this isn't purple, it's eggplant.

Sure, Mom. Chicks dig a dude who's sporting the latest eggplant turtleneck styles.

I grabbed any old black shirt off of the floor, stalked past my mom as I pulled it on, and went downstairs. Jeffrey was sitting on the couch looking miserable, but he had enough energy to embarrass me in front of my mom.

Do you think RENEE ALBERT will dance with you, Steven? You think she's HOT, right?

Oh, leave me alone, shrimp boy. Renee Albert has a boyfriend.

Will you dance with ANNETTE? She's pretty, too. And she knows you're alive.

Where does he GET this stuff? *I don't know, Jeffrey. Usually there's a big line of girls waiting to dance with me, so it depends on how soon Annette gets there. There's just not a big enough supply of Steven Alper around to meet the demand.*

That's a joke, right?

Yeah, it's a joke. I'll probably just stand in the corner, trying not to be noticed, until the decoration committee accidentally packs me into a box at the end of the night. There I will lie, crammed between rolls of crepe paper, until the New Year's dance two months from now.

Jeffrey thought about this for a moment, and said, *Won't they notice the box is too heavy when they go to put it away?*

Good point, Jeffrey.

Steven, put your brother's shoes on, will you? We have to get moving.

They'll never fit me, Mom.

Har, har, very funny. Now let's GO!

It wasn't until we were all in the car, several blocks away from home, that I realized the random shirt I had put on was last year's middle school band concert shirt. Perfect. It was easier than building and carrying a giant picket sign with the word "Geek" on it, but it achieved the exact same effect!

When we pulled up at school, I was pretty distracted, but I did notice that Jeffrey didn't look so great. I came up with a new bargain with God: "If you make Jeffrey better, I won't go to this dance." Maybe God knew that right then, staying out of the dance didn't feel like a big sacrifice to me, because he didn't instantly cure my brother. I ruffled Jeffrey's hair, told him to be good and not to play too much WWF Wrestling Live with his fragile mother, took a deep breath, and walked away into my big night.

Inside the dance, I found a bunch of my friends

standing around in a corner. It suddenly struck me that the two worst social situations in middle school — dances and dodgeball — had a lot in common for guys like me. You go to the gym, stand in a corner as far away from the action as possible, and try not to be seen. Your eyes scan the room for threats — either flying projectiles aimed at your head or girls aimed at mortifying you by getting you out on the floor — and you sweat profusely while standing still. Also, you're wearing clothing that embarrasses you, and you feel like everybody else is better at this game than you are. And in both situations, you desperately hope that some miracle will occur to bring you glory, but you're too scared to attempt to do anything that might actually achieve any recognition.

Oh yeah, dances and dodgeball: the two Ds of my middle school nightmares.

Of course, looking around was kind of fun. Renee Albert was looking incredible in some kind of tight-ish shiny thing, and her little court of supergirls were all dancing together, flipping their hair around and occasionally stopping to do little fix-up things with their sparkly lip gloss. I remember wondering how I could be so awkward about this stuff, but these girls — raised in the same town as me, with basically the same exact social experiences I had — could be so cool.

Then Annette came bounding over to me. She was wearing jeans and a shirt like I was, but somehow the fact that we were at a dance made me too aware that she was female, so I felt weird talking with her. Plus, all of my guy friends were standing around, smirking.

Hi, Steven.

Hi, Annette.

Did you listen to that CD?

Uhhh . . . yeah.

Did you figure it out?

Uhhh . . . I did. And I have a drum lesson with Mr. Stoll tomorrow. I think I'll bring it along so I can work on it with him.

OK, make sure you do, because I have big plans for you.

You do?

She just smiled and walked away. "Perfect!" I thought. "The girl of my dreams has no idea I'm in the room, even though I've sat behind her in every class since first grade, and Annette has 'big plans' for me."

I stood around for a while more, listening to my friends' moronic commentary about how Annette wanted to jump on me and make me her band-geek love slave, until my night took the final plunge into horror. My mother walked in. I didn't see her at first, and I guess she didn't spot me, so she had to get the DJ to stop the music and announce that Steven Alper's mother was here to pick him up.

Right on the spot, without knowing what exactly was going on, I made God one final offer. "Take me. Don't take Jeffy. Please, Lord. Take *me*."

FEVER

If you've never been dragged out of a middle school dance by your mom while she's wearing sweatpants and carrying your pajama-clad little brother over her shoulder, then you haven't had the same kind of life I'm leading this year.

As she rushed me to the car at breakneck speed, my mom told me what was going on. *We're going to the emergency room. Your brother has a fever.*

I looked at the top of Jeffrey's sleeping head, and even in the dim school hallway lights I could see that his hair was all matted with sweat.

Why is that an emergency? What does it mean? Where's Dad?

Dad is still at his dinner. I don't know the name of the restaurant, and his cell phone must be turned off. Any time your brother gets a fever from now on, it's an emergency. I don't know what this means. Get the doors, please.

OK. Mom, is this serious?

I don't know, honey. I don't know. I wish I knew.

She must have thought the situation was pretty urgent, though, because she usually won't leave the house in sweats, and I noticed she hadn't even taken the time to put shoes on Jeffrey. Also, she's the careful driver in our family on most days, but our ride to the hospital was like the Indy 500. I didn't even have time to think of how in the world I was going to explain this away to my friends on Monday — I was mostly too busy trying to keep from passing out from the incredible g-forces every time we turned a corner. Somehow, Jeffrey didn't wake up, but he was definitely groaning in his sleep. I reached over and crammed his blanket between his head and the corner of his booster seat so he wouldn't get whipped around so much; my hand brushed against his forehead, and he was definitely ragingly hot.

The E.R. staff didn't mess around at all when we got there. As soon as my mom said the word "leukemia," there were doctors, nurses, and technicians swarming all over. The doctor in charge was barking orders like a Marine drill sergeant, with questions in between for my mom.

We'll need a CBC and full differential. Do you know what his last counts were? When were those taken? Does he have a catheter? What kind? Take his shirt off. OK, access the Port-a-Cath. Make a note — we'll need to run some heparin soon. Get the bloods first — we have to have those numbers.

As they started to take Jeffrey's clothes off, he woke up. I guess he wasn't surprised to find himself in a hospital — both he and my mother seemed to have become used to this bizarre world. I couldn't even understand what the doctors and nurses were saying, but they were both clued in to this secret language. He didn't say anything as they took his temperature orally, even though he used to always make a big show of choking when my parents did it at home. He responded to all of the commands that came his way — *Tilt your head! Take three deep breaths! Lean forward, please!* — with mute obedience. Until they laid him down, and went for his chest with a needle. Now, I knew that something had been done to Jeffrey's chest in Philadelphia; I had seen the two lines of stitches and the round bulge under the skin of his ribs. But during the whole period up until that night, the medical stuff had only sunk in to a point; I only accepted what I had to accept to make sense of any given moment. So I only really knew that he was taking steroids every day, for example, when I saw him gagging down the syringes of bitter liquid in the kitchen every morning and night. And I guess now was my moment to believe in the Port-a-Cath, which was an IV tube that had been surgically implanted under the skin a couple of inches above Jeffrey's right nipple.

Jeffrey pulled away from the doctor when he saw the needle and asked in a little pathetic voice, *Can't we do the emm-luh?*

I didn't know it then, but EMLA is a cream that makes your skin numb. They had been using EMLA so Jeffrey wouldn't feel the hurt of the needle as it stabbed through his skin to get at the catheter in his chest.

The doctor's voice softened then, and he almost whispered to Jeffrey, *I'm sorry, buddy. The EMLA takes an hour to work, and we can't wait.*

Then the doctor half-turned to me, and asked Jeffrey, *Would it help if your brother held your hand?*

Jeffrey didn't respond at all, but he looked at me, and his eyes were brimming. I am pretty squeamish about shots and blood and stuff, but what was I going to do? I grabbed his hand and let him sort of lean his head on my shoulder without sitting up from his pillow. I started the "You're OK, Jeffy" chant, and a nurse scrubbed the circle of skin over the port with yellowish-orange stuff. Then she broke open one of those sterile packets that needles come in and took out a truly large one, which was bent in the middle at a ninety-degree angle. Jeffrey started to whimper, and the tears began to soak the shoulder of my shirt, but he didn't even flinch as the huge needle jabbed straight into his chest. The nurse taped the needle in place, and I closed my eyes. I heard someone say, "Flushing the port," and then I got a little woozy. Jeffrey kept squeezing my hand really hard for a few minutes, until the blood specimens had all been taken and an IV line was hooked up to his port.

I think we both fell asleep for a little while.

When I opened my eyes, the doctor was talking with my mom; neither of them noticed I was awake, so I just lay there and listened. Evidently, Jeffrey had what should have been a simple ear infection, but his white blood cell counts were low because of the chemotherapy drugs he was on, so his body couldn't fight off germs very well. The doctor was saying that Jeffrey would need to spend a few days in the hospital, getting antibiotics through his IV line in addition to his regular chemo medicines. My mom didn't look pleased.

Can we do this here, or does he —

He'll be here until the morning. We'll put him on a pediatric floor for now, but we're going to have to transport him to Children's Hospital in Philadelphia as soon as his fever is down.

Transport him?

Yes, we can send him in an ambulance, so we don't have to stop his IV, or we can cap the line and have you drive him. I'll consult with the specialists down there in the morning, and whatever they want to do —

Oh, God. How expensive is an ambulance ride?

I don't know, but we have to do whatever is best for your son medically right now.

I understand. We're just having some financial trouble with all of this. I've had to leave my job and . . . My mom started crying then. *I'm sorry, Doctor. I just . . . it's all been so sudden, you know? We have very good insurance. But this all adds up: the co-pays, parking, food, gas, tolls. And my husband isn't really . . . taking it well, yet.*

I hear you, Ma'am. He sort of patted my mom on the shoulder at this point. *I'll be back around in a few hours. We'll be moving you all up to a private room any minute now, and then maybe you can try and get some rest.*

Yeah, sure. My mom looked tired enough to sleep for a week, but I knew she wasn't going to get any rest.

I got out of Jeffrey's bed for the big move upstairs, and fell back asleep in a chair by the window of the new room. My mom spent a few hours lying on a cot they had brought in, but I really don't think you could say she slept. Every hour or so some medical person or other came in to take Jeffrey's temperature or attach a new bag to his IV or do something that would ruin our rest.

At 2 a.m., my mom walked out of the room. I wanted to know what was going on, so after a couple of minutes, I followed her. I found her sitting in the hallway, leaning back on the wall with her knees to her chest, holding a cup of coffee that must have come from the little coin-operated machine that was out there. I plopped down next to her.

Hey, Mom. How are ya?

I'm fine, Steven. I was really worried about your brother last night, but it looks like this is just . . . going . . . to be what life is like for a while.

Mom, how long is this all going to last?

They're going to run some tests next week. If he's cancer-free by then, he'll still be in treatment for a few years. Then, who knows? After five years without cancer, he should be totally normal.

Mom, what if he's not cancer-free next week?

I don't know, Steven. I just don't know. By the way, I'm sorry we ruined your night.

Mom, forget it. It was fine.

Oh, really? Fine, was it? Should I storm into your graduation wearing sweats, too?

Yeah, that would be pretty cool. Maybe you could have your hair up in curlers for extra style points?

I might be able to swing that, Stevie. And how about some flip-flops on my feet?

Excellent, Mom. That would be excellent.

Right there in the hallway, I put my head in her lap. She stroked my hair for a while, and then she sent me back into the room.

Get some sleep, pal.

At about 5:00 in the morning, my dad came into the room and shook me awake (I guess my mom had gotten through to him by phone at some point). He put a finger over his lips so I wouldn't make noise and wake Jeffrey, but, of course, right when I was about to tiptoe out of the room, a lady came crashing in with the giant breakfast cart. So we had this odd little family conference while Jeffrey attempted to choke down some food. My parents spent a few minutes looking at Jeffrey's hospital chart, worked out the details of what needed to be done if my mom and Jeffrey were going to Philadelphia for a week, and went out into the hall to argue about something. I had a little while alone with Jeffrey. He looked really exhausted, but his fever was gone, and he was much more alert mentally than he'd been the night before. He asked me about my dance. *Did you have fun? Did you dance a lot? Did Renee Albert kiss you? Did it feel gross?*

Get out of here, you little nutball. I'm telling you, I have zero chance of kissing Renee Albert. Zero. Zilch. Nada.

So who DID you kiss?

Nobody. I was just standing around with my friends when you came to get me.

Did I ruin your night?

Mom asked me that, too. Jeffy, you didn't ruin my night. It was ruined from the start. You had a worse night than I did, anyway.

Oh, well. At least you didn't have to kiss anybody.

Yes, Jeffy, that's a big comfort to me.

My parents came back in, and I started to get up and leave. Jeffrey asked me for a hug, and I gave him one.

Take care, Jeffy. I'll see you soon, right? Just remember not to throw food at the nurses. I don't want to get any complaint calls, OK?

Steven, I don't throw food at . . . oh, that was a joke, right?

Yup, buddy boy. It was a joke. But seriously, no kissing the nurses on their lips, either. It messes up their makeup.

Eeeeeeewwwww!

It was about 7 a.m. when my dad and I got home. I somehow made it to my bed and collapsed into a near-coma that lasted until I got too hungry to sleep through lunchtime. It was probably noon or so when I made it to the kitchen. My dad was sitting there, looking stubbly and worn-down, eating a bagel without much of an expression on his face. He gave me a tiny nod that was almost businesslike — totally neutral, like he wasn't really seeing me. I got out cereal and milk, and it was so quiet between us that I was getting grossed out by the distinct sounds of our food-chewing processes. As soon as I finished, I went downstairs to play the drums. And play the drums. And play the drums. I played through all of the basic rudiments and then did all of my lesson pages for the week. Then I put five CDs in the changer behind my drums, put on my headphones, pressed SHUFFLE, and played along with at least ten really loud metal songs in a row without stopping.

I looked up in the middle of a Led Zeppelin drum solo, and my dad was sitting on the beat-up old couch about 8 feet in front of my bass drum. Because he startled me pretty badly and because I figured he was probably about 43% deaf if he had been sitting there a while, I jumped up and whipped off the headphones.

Uhhh . . . hi, Dad.

I just got the call from your mother. They're taking Jeffrey to Philadelphia in about two hours. She wants us to get his stuff together for him. Do you know what toys and clothes he likes? Can you help me? My dad looked ashamed, like he had asked me to steal him a bottle of Jack Daniel's or something.

Sure, Dad.

Hey, you've been down here playing for a while now. Are you all right?

I couldn't believe my father was just now noticing me, and that I might be upset about my brother's situation. *I'm fine, Dad.*

Oh, your mother thought you seemed upset at the emergency room and when they put the tubes in . . .

Dad, they didn't just put tubes in. They stabbed him in the chest. They STABBED him!

I was stunned by what happened next, although I had to admit it was becoming a pretty common occurrence: I started to cry. And once I started, I couldn't stop. My dad wasn't necessarily going to win the Teddy Bear Society's Father of the Year Award, but for the first time in weeks, he reacted. He put his arm around my shoulders and sort of squeezed me in. We must have stayed like that for a good twenty minutes, until I couldn't postpone blowing my nose anymore. I picked my head up off of my dad, walked over to the other end of the sofa, got a tissue, and blew my nose. Then I sat right back down next to him. We stared at each other without having any concept of what to do or say next. My dad finally broke the silence with an old family punch line.

So, umm, how about those Knicks?

We chuckled awkwardly, but at least it was a chuckle. Then we went upstairs and packed up Jeffrey's stuff. On the drive over to the hospital, I had an odd realization: This was the first time in weeks that I had laughed with each member of my family within a 24-hour period.

At the hospital, Jeffrey was looking fairly worried. My mom was out in the hall, arguing with the doctors in Philly on her cell phone. My dad stayed to talk with her, and I went right to my brother.

Hey, Jeffy, how ya feelin'?

I'm OK. We had moatmeal for breakfast, but it wasn't as good as yours. I'm scared.

What are you scared about?

Mommy said that they might have to do another

bone narrow tomorrow. It was supposed to be next time, but now it's tomorrow. The bone narrow HURTS. And I might still be very sick if they give it to me early. They said they would do it in a month and all the bad blasts should be gone. But what if they aren't gone yet? Then they have to give me more throw-up medicine. It's NO FAIR!

Jeffy, I'm sure the doctors know what they're doing. They wouldn't do the bone-marrow test early unless they thought it would be OK.

But it might not be OK. It might really really not.

Well, buddy, you're in luck. Check out what I brought you.

And with a flourish, I pulled his favorite Rescue Heroes action figure out of his bag.

Look! It's Matt Medic. He's here to protect you.

Matt Medic, I'm scared.

Don't be frightened, young man.

He always loved it when I pretended to be one of his toys, and Matt Medic was perfect for the occasion. He carries a huge plastic paramedic pack and a giant gunlike thing that we always pretended was some kind of vaccine syringe.

But what if I'm still very sick?

Well, son, just concentrate on my Matt Medic Shot Shooter. It's full of magic antiblast gas — guaranteed to save your bone marrow. Here we go.

And I used Matt Medic to give Jeffrey a "shot."

That ought to do it. Just remember, you never have to worry when Matt Medic's on the job. And one other thing: Don't kiss the nurses. It gets them in trouble!

My parents came into the room then, and we had the whole obligatory hugs-and-farewells scene. It was fairly touching, all things considered. We said we'd be back together again soon and that everything would be fine, and at that moment, everyone in the family was united toward the common goal of getting Jeffrey well.

The last thing I said to Jeffrey was, *I'll see you in no time, pal. Just remember to listen to Matt Medic, and there will be no trouble!* As things would turn out, though, there would be a lot more of both time and trouble before we were all in one room again.

TROUBLE

While I was waiting for the school bus on Monday, I had a horrifying realization: People were going to ask me why my mom had pulled me out of the dance on Friday night. By the time the bus pulled up at my stop, I was convinced that as soon as I got on, all eyes would immediately swing to the front, pinning me in the merciless glare of massed teenage inquisition. Of course, nobody even looked my way. Renee Albert went running onto the bus right before me, and you just don't get a lot of attention if you're walking behind Renee Albert. A 7-foot-tall Mickey Mouse could have slipped on in between us, but all anyone would have seen was Renee's outfit or her new hair or the gigantic charm bracelet Biff had given her when he met her after the dance.

So I was OK. I sat down alone in a seat, with my head kind of tucked down into my sweatshirt. It was a really stupid and pointless defense, like when a turtle tucks into its shell because a locomotive is barreling down on it. In my case, Annette was the locomotive.

She came over to me and completely ignored the fact that I was trying to burrow my way through the bottom of my seat and into the luggage compartment.

Hi, Steven. Are you all right? I was worried about you all weekend. Is everything OK at your house? My mom said she saw "Get Well" balloons tied to your mailbox the other day. Or are you in trouble for something? Did your parents find out you skipped out of math last week? If that's what it is, I'm so sorry. It's all my fault. I'll tell them if you want me to. It's . . .

Annette! This has nothing to do with you. It's a family thing, and I'm fine. I'm fine.

So you're not mad at . . .

I SAID I'm fine.

OK, I was just asking. You've changed lately, though.

I have NOT changed lately.

Yes, you have. You never do your work anymore, you space out all day unless you're in band, and you yell at me half the time when I try to talk to you.

Oh, yeah? If I've changed so much, how come no one else has noticed anything?

Well, I just think . . .

I'm serious, Annette. Nothing's wrong. Everything's perfectly normal. I'm just . . . tired of school, that's all. And my mom picked me up because we had to go somewhere. You have to give me credit for that last one — I didn't lie to her.

All right, Steven. Whatever.

So how was your weekend, Annette? Did you practice a lot? Are you going to be ready for Juilliard?

I thought for sure I could distract her by starting a discussion about the whole piano-genius thing, but it didn't entirely work. She knew something was up, and even if she couldn't immediately tie me down and administer truth serum on a yellow bus in the middle of South Main Street, I could see in her eyes that she was wanting to wrestle the info out of me somehow.

Well, the keyboard-themed small talk smoothed over the end of the bus ride, anyhow.

I made it through homeroom without speaking to anybody and was just settling in for a nice period of off-topic journal writing in Miss Palma's class when the intercom blared, calling me to the office.

As I was walking out of class, I could feel two pairs of eyes pinned on me. Miss Palma gave me a sad, sympathetic look, and Annette was studying me like she was Sherlock Holmes and I was a handkerchief at a crime scene.

The school secretaries told me to walk through the front office into the guidance area. Whatever was about to happen to me apparently had a mental-health angle — I had become what my mom refers to as a "student concern." The counselor waved me right into her cubicle-y office and gestured toward a seat. I had never been there before, but I got the vibe pretty fast — if you're into pastels and motivational posters, that little cube was definitely the place to be.

Steven, my name is Mrs. Galley. I called you down today because some of your teachers are concerned about you.

Something about this situation got my inner smart-mouthed child going.

I would kinda hope all of my teachers are concerned about me. But if you would kindly tell me which ones aren't, maybe I could buy them some apples or something?

Steven, I think you know what I mean. You're here because you have apparently stopped doing work in your major subjects. You've never been in any kind of trouble here before, but you're suddenly in danger of failing everything across the board. Can you talk to me about why that might be?

Well, truthfully, Mrs. Galley, you may have heard about the worldwide pencil shortage. I like to think that by skipping my homework, I'm doing my little bit to conserve.

Then she did something that generally works pretty well on me: She administered the Silent Treatment. She just looked and looked at me. I tried desperately to occupy my attention by looking at other things in the office: the little poster with all the different smiley emotion faces on it, the stuffed-animal Garfield on top of the filing cabinet, the jar of candy hearts on the desk. The candy hearts did it, in a way — they distracted me from Mrs. Galley's stare, but they also made me really want to eat one of them. After the high-powered battle of wills reached an unbearable peak of tension, I asked for a candy heart.

You want a candy heart, huh?

Yes, Mrs. Galley.

Well, I have a little rule here, Steven. You talk, you eat.

I began to realize, perhaps too late, that I had underestimated this lady. The silence fell over us again. I was not ready to tell anyone about Jeffrey. And after three weeks of keeping this secret in, I was darned well not going to crack over a stupid piece of penny candy.

Just then, the bell rang.

OK, I guess I'll just be going now. It was nice meeting you. Thanks for nearly giving me some candy.

HOLD ON, Steven. You have gym this period, don't you?

Yes. Why?

Did you ever wonder what all of your subject teachers do second period, if every single student on your team has gym?

Well, ummm, not really. Do they hang out behind the shop room and smoke unfiltered Camels?

Nope. They all meet with each other. In fact, they're meeting right now. And you and I are going to head on down there and meet WITH them.

Do we have to?

Yup.

Do we REALLY have to?

Uh-huh.

I started to walk out of her office on the little Walk of Doom she had arranged for me.

Not so fast, Steven.

I whirled back around.

Want a candy heart?

OK, I wasn't feeling too proud at the moment. I took a candy heart, and the long walk began.

When we walked in, all of my major-subject teachers were sitting around a huge conference table, drinking coffee, laughing, grading papers. They looked up at me without any surprise on their faces: I had been set up, for sure. Mrs. Galley led me to a seat and sat down next to me. Next, the teachers started in. Here's what I heard:

Steven, we like you . . . blah, blah.

And you've always been an excellent yada yada.

But suddenly you're not performing up to your hmrf hmrf hmrf.

Your grade in my class has slipped from a ninety-two to a hurga hurga hurga.

We're here today so that you can help us understand how to help you with nonny nonny nonny.

Steven? Can you tell us what has been going on?

Steven?

STEE-VEN?

Ummm . . . there's nothing going on. I've just been busy. You know, with band, and jazz band, and All-City High School Jazz Band. So, uhhh, I just haven't . . . haven't been home much.

At that precise moment, Mr. Watras walked in. What — do these people have psychic powers or something?

Steven, I'm concerned about your grades, too. Your

teachers asked me to be here today, because if things don't improve, you might not be eligible to practice or perform with the All-City group.

I was thinking, "Hey, Mr. W. — where's all your 'Dude' and 'Cat' lingo? Now all of a sudden, just because we're in a big meeting, you're like Mr. Teacher Man?" But I didn't have too long to concentrate on this particular betrayal, because Mrs. Galley chimed in again.

Steven, nobody wants to punish you, but we need to get to the bottom of this drastic change in your attitude and habits, and we need a commitment from you to do your work. I'll ask you again, is there anything that we should know?

No, I'm just . . . it's just . . .

And then all of a sudden, I got choked up — which, of course, was becoming a pattern with me. And I started to be honest — which hadn't been my pattern for a while.

My brother . . . my brother . . .

While I paused to cry and my math teacher passed me a box of tissues — do all the kids crack

like robins' eggs when they get hauled in here? —
Miss Palma said, *Tell them, Steven.*

Not "Tell us, Steven," but "Tell them, Steven."
Which meant she knew.

My brother . . . has cancer.

Boy, if you ever want to shut up a room full of
grown-ups, evidently "My brother has cancer" is the
secret command code. They all just looked at me in
silence for a good fifteen seconds. Well, not a *good*
fifteen seconds, but you know what I mean. Even as I
tried to blow my nose and wipe my eyes on the thin,
crappy school tissue without looking too horren-
dously gross, I was thinking, "Why do these people
basically beat the truth out of you if they don't want
to hear it?"

When they did start talking again, their tone was
a lot softer and gentler. Mr. Watras said that, of
course, under the circumstances, I could stay in All-
City — provided that I started to do my work again.
Each subject teacher agreed to put together a packet
for me to do as makeup work, and they went so far
as to give me the Christmas break to get the papers

in, because the marking period would be over in January. Mrs. Galley even gave me another candy heart. But there was one more item on my agenda.

Do my parents have to know about this? If I swear I'll make up all the work on time, can you wait to call them? My mom is with my brother at the hospital, and my dad is really . . . upset right now. I'll do every bit of work, I promise. Can I please just have a chance?

Everyone agreed to that, and the meeting was adjourned just as the period ended. I wasn't ready to walk out into a school hallway yet, so I took my time, using up some more tissues and taking a series of very, very deep breaths. Miss Palma stayed behind with me for a minute.

Steven, if there's anything else I can do —

You read my journal, didn't you?

No, I didn't read your journal. What do you mean?

You knew my brother had — you knew about my brother.

Steven, I assure you, I didn't read your journal. I never read anything a student doesn't want me to, ever.

Then how did you know?

Other . . . people know about your brother's condition.

Who?

Steven, we're both going to be late to our third-period classes.

Who? Who knew? Who told you?

A student, Steven. A student came to me because she was extremely worried about you and didn't know what to do.

Annette. I was going to have to go to the bathroom during math class and have a talk with that girl.

For the next couple of periods plus lunch, I sat around worrying about how much work I was going to have to make up and fuming about how Annette had known my secret all along. And not told me. AND told a teacher!

Then it was math time. I got permission to leave the room with no trouble. Even though I had skipped out after going to the bathroom the week before, no teacher was about to deny me anything on this particular day. Just so I would know I hadn't been lying completely, I did go to the bathroom on my way to the band room. Even from there, I could hear that

Annette was playing something really fast and angry-sounding, which was like a perfect soundtrack for my mood. I followed the sounds and burst into the room so hard that Annette stopped playing and jumped up.

Hi, Steven. Are you OK?

Yes, I'm fine. I'm more than fine — I'm peachy. I love getting led into a teacher meeting and dragged over the coals by half the grown-ups in the school because SOME GIRL ratted me out.

What are you talking about?

Oh, like you don't know? I'm talking about how you ran and told Miss Palma.

Told her what?

About Jeffrey's cancer!

Annette stood dead still and looked as though I had slapped her.

Jeffrey has cancer?

Oh, my God. You didn't . . . know?

As awkward moments go, this one just took the cake. Annette was clearly stunned by this news. Now I was in the strange position of comforting her about my brother's deadly illness. I must have said something right, though, because after a few minutes she stopped being so sad about Jeffrey and started being furious at me for not telling her. To make a long story short, she pretty much lectured me for about ten minutes, until I realized I had to get back to math. I knew I had to end this fiasco of a conversation.

Thanks for your sympathy in my time of pain, Annette.

I turned to storm out and heard her shouting after me.

Steven, wait!

But I never stopped walking away. I knew I was being unreasonable, but I had taken a lot of abuse already that day, and I just was not going to make peace with anyone at the moment.

When I was halfway back to my classroom, a weird thought occurred to me: If Annette hadn't told Miss Palma, then who had?

Of course, when I walked back into math class I got a big look from the teacher, but it wasn't the withering one I would have gotten the week before. Instead it was the same kind of semi-pitying, semi-trying-to-be-cheerful grimace that all of our home visitors had pasted onto their faces just as they rang our doorbell. I went back to my seat and actually paid attention until the end of the period. On my way out the door, the teacher handed me a huge folder: the worksheets I would need to do as catch-up work. He might have been my fastest-moving teacher, but his approach wasn't unique. By the end of the next day, I was carting around five of these fun packs in an alarming assortment of pastel and Day-Glo colors.

Anyway, I went to other classes, played some drums, and walked out to the bus. Annette got on after I did but didn't come over to sit next to me. Instead, yet another bizarre event came crashing into my day — Renee sashayed onto the bus, looked around until she locked eyes with me, and took Annette's empty seat.

Hi, Steven.

Uhhh . . . hi, Renee. Can I . . . ummm . . . help you with something?

You might notice what a smooth talker I was. I'd lived around the corner from this girl since we were, like, embryos, but that was the best response I could come up with. Amazing.

Well, I . . . ummm . . . my mom ran into your mom at Shop Rite last week and . . .

Yeah?

I'm sorry about your brother.

My brother?

You know? About his being sick and all? This must be really hard for you.

No, I'm OK. Really. It's no big deal.

Your mom says Jeffrey's being really brave about this.

Yeah, well, we're fine.

You know what, Steven? You're brave, too.

I am? (I am? I don't feel brave. I feel like a galloping idiot, stumbling from crisis to crisis, barely able to speak to any normal person, much less Renee Albert.)

You are. I knew something was wrong. I even . . .

You even what?

I even . . . I hope you're not mad.

Then she did this little lip-biting thing she always does, which always makes me think about kissing her for some reason. I looked away for a minute, because being so attracted to Renee made it hard to concentrate on what she was saying. Annette, sitting a few seats up and to the left, was glaring at me. I didn't have time to ponder that too deeply, though, because Renee spoke again.

I even . . . I told Miss Palma about Jeffrey.

Holy cow. Renee Albert knew I was alive. But I wished I were dead.

STARVING IN SIBERIA

Time passed. Jeffrey came home. Winter blew into town with full force. Somewhere in there was a very strange Christmas, where Jeffrey got a mound of presents that was nearly taller than our tree. Relatives flew in from every corner of the country, but nobody smiled much. Meanwhile, I did worksheets. Lots and lots of worksheets.

At home, I was worried that my parents would notice the massive amount of work I was cranking out, wonder about it, comment on it. But on the days Mom was in Philly, Dad was still in mute mode, and when Mom was back, she slept and my dad spent time with Jeffrey. I seriously think I could have sat in the middle of the kitchen floor rubbing two sticks together over a pile of dynamite blocks and gasoline cans, and my parents would have been oblivious, as long as I was keeping myself occupied. What nobody was tuning into was that there's a big difference between keeping myself occupied and actually taking care of myself.

And I was angry. Mindlessly, relentlessly angry every minute of every day. I did all the work my teachers gave me, and I did it well, but I was so tense while I was doing it that I broke mounds of pencils, erased right through the paper repeatedly, left indentations on my desktop from writing so hard. Word got out at school about my "tragic situation," and I was like a mini-celebrity. Renee was instantly my pal, and Annette forgave me, as usual. Teachers were thrilled with my "great new attitude" and kept telling me what a "trooper" I was. On the rare occasions when they noticed my presence, my relatives commented about how "strong" and "brave" I was, about how "lucky" Jeffrey was to have me for a brother. Why didn't they try being "lucky" like Jeffrey for a few months?

And I wanted to scream at every teacher, "Why are you making me do this stupid busywork while my brother's white cell count is so low? Who cares about listing the first ten presidents when my brother has another spinal tap on Friday? What possible use is the FOIL method of multiplying binomials when my brother's gums are bleeding every time he tries to brush his teeth?"

And I wanted to punch every kid who told me they "understood" my pain. *Nobody* understood my pain. Maybe if I had gone to each of their houses, whacking random family members with a nail-studded two-by-four, they would have begun to have some basic comprehension.

And my parents — they were trying ... but GOD! I couldn't even look at them without having to bite my tongue.

Meanwhile, Jeffrey went bald. He lost his beautiful, golden hair. Soft ringlets were all over his pillow, the shoulders of his favorite Buzz Lightyear PJs, the bathroom sink. And then one day, there was just nothing left to fall out. For a long time, he never said anything to me about it, but between that and the swelling in his face from all the steroids he was taking, he was looking horrible.

Of course, the steroids also made him hyper beyond all belief, so even while he was the only person I wasn't mad at yet, he was driving me pretty crazy. He wasn't able to go to school for weeks on end when his white blood cell counts were low, so I was basically his sole source of entertainment. A typical weeknight when he was home went like this:

1. Sit down and try to do homework.
2. Get interrupted by Jeffrey: "Please play with me!"
3. Ignore brother, try to do homework.
4. Get interrupted by Jeffrey: "Come ON, Steven! I'm BORED!"
5. Beg Jeffrey for five minutes of peace.
6. Get begged for five minutes of play: "Steven, you never, ever play with me — ever!"
7. Move entire homework operations center to different room.
8. Repeat steps #1–7 as directed by small, drugged maniac.

I did play with him for at least an hour each night, but a lot of times, neither of us was concentrating too much on the games. I was constantly hoping for an excuse to stop playing, and Jeffrey often wasn't feeling well. It was like Checkers Nite at the Terminal Boredom and Nausea Clinic.

Also, if anyone out there ever wants to experience the ultimate in crippling guilt, I recommend that you try beating a bald, bloated five-year-old cancer patient at a board game. So to avoid the guilt, I would spend half my time sneakily cheating so that Jeffrey would win over and over.

Which also sucked, because the more he won, the more he wanted to play.

There's another thing for which I will feel guilty forever: Jeffrey was driving me so nuts with his need for attention that I was often relieved when he went back into the hospital. I mean, I needed the time off from him so I could catch up on schoolwork, but how hideous was that? I wished for my own baby brother to be hospitalized just so I wouldn't have to play some one-sided Chutes and Ladders games.

I had a moment of triumph in January when I finally handed in my last overdue worksheet. I wrote about it in English class and even read the journal out loud. Here's the conclusion of the day's entry:

My fellow students, I stand here before you a changed man. Once I lived in fear, sneaking from place to place, avoiding schoolwork at all costs. My life was a tangled mass of lies and half-truths. And I thought I could get away with it. I thought I could carry on indefinitely with my schemes and deceptions. I thought I would be able to leave my homework undone forever. But I was wrong — oh, so very wrong. Friends, there exists on this planet a delicate balance, a balance between good and evil, righteousness and wretchedness, crime and punishment. And when any one man tries to tip the scales too far, they always bounce back. Beware. BEWARE!

• • •

Okay, so the journal prompt was "Pick any character in Mark Twain's works and explain how he or she is changed by his or her experiences." Miss Palma did commend me on my "rhetorical flair," though. And that's gotta count for something.

So my work was made up. My 'rents wouldn't be getting the dreaded phone call from Mrs. Galley. I could stay in All-City. And it looked as though my school worries were over. But who are we kidding here? Nobody knows how to get slapped down by fate like Steven Alper. Just when things were turning around, I got the flu.

Big whoop, right? Sweat a little, barf a little, lie in bed watching videos for a few days while the 'rents wait on you hand and foot — not a bad deal, overall. However, if you have a brother with leukemia who needs to avoid exposure to viruses, you can't BE in the same HOUSE as your parents when you have the flu. So, just when I needed my parents the most, in my hour of deepest need and intestinal crampage, they shipped me off across town to my grampa and grandma's.

Now, I love my grampa as much as I love anybody — and my grandma is all right, too, when she's not dusting around me every five minutes or nagging me about my posture — but their house is, to put it mildly, primitive. Do they have a VCR? No. DVD player? Nope. CD player? Negatory. Computer? No. PlayStation? Uh-uh.

It was like my parents had sent their diseased eldest child to Siberia.

I spent a total of eight days in that glorified hut, but I mostly just slept the first few away. The last five were the problem. How many games of Go Fish can a normal thirteen-year-old boy play with his grandma without suffering permanent brain damage? Hopefully, the limit is more than the seventeen in a row I played with mine. How long can that same normal boy talk with his grandfather without running out of meaningful things to say? The answer to that is four days, IF the boy is essentially comatose for the first three of them. And how weird does my grandparents' house smell, by the way? Once my nose started clearing up on Day Five, my nausea got even worse, because that odd aroma of old pot roast mixed with mothballs was nobody's idea of a stomach soother.

Speaking of pot roast, I had spent the three months before this involuntary visit subsisting only by a combination of my wits and the microwave. You would think that this week of having actual food, prepared by a human cook, would have been a welcome change. However, despite the lingering meat fumes, my grandma never fed me anything other than bananas, rice, applesauce, and toast, in consideration of my illness. Gggrrrrrr! It got so bad that I actually spent hours lying on the couch watching Grandma knit, plotting ways to sneak into the kitchen and steal some meat.

How pathetic is that? A week with the grand-'rents and I was desperate enough to contemplate the vile crime of beef felony. Another few days and I would have probably gotten scurvy or goiter or something.

There were some good things about that week, though. Lack of school attendance comes to mind as the biggest treat, although I was worried about having more makeup work to do and about failing my finals. I got lots of phone calls from my mom and Jeffrey, and they even dropped stuff off in my grand-'rents' mailbox for me. The nicest one was a present from Jeffrey with a note my mom must have told him how to spell.

> Dear Steven,
>
> I'm sorry you are so sick. I sent Matt Medic to help you get better. When he gives you a magic flu-blaster shot, make sure you think strong no-flu thoughts. Doctor Purow said that's important.
>
> Also, Mommy told Daddy you sound like you're about to die. If you promise you will get better instead of dying, I promise I will, too.
>
> Your pal,
>
> Jeffrey Alper

Good thing he put his last name on there, huh?

I also got some surprise phone calls; I guess my parents were giving everyone my grandparents' number in the hopes that they would all call and save me from a slow, agonizing death by malnutrition and gin rummy. Annette called me twice, a couple of the guys from school left messages, and Mr. Watras and Miss Palma each called once. It was exceptionally strange talking on the phone with teachers. I mean, I was lying there in ratty sweatpants, amid a vast sea of soggy tissues. It couldn't have been a pretty mental picture. Mr. Watras asked me whether I was practicing, and I told him I was practicing my tissue basketball skills. Then I got all embarrassed. I mean, I know teachers are people, or at least most of them are, but you don't usually talk with them exactly like you talk with everybody else. Still, any call that got me away from watching *All in the Family* and *Golden Girls* with Grandma for the third straight evening was an A-OK call in my book.

By the end of the week, I was still kind of hurt by the fact that I had been exiled. I mean, I knew exactly why it had to happen, but it still gets to you when your brother is all cozied up at home with both parents and you're stuck sucking down applesauce with the mah-jongg crowd way across town. I wanted attention from the 'rents, and I wanted it big-time.

Also, I was having these bizarre dreams about hunting down wild game with my bare hands. I had to get back into a diet with some protein, and fast. So that Sunday, I bade farewell to my grandma and got into the huge cruise ship that is Grampa's car for the ride back to my actual life.

But silly me! I was forgetting that I didn't have an actual life. Thus, when I got home, the banners, flags, and tumbling cheerleaders that should have been lining the curb to celebrate my return were notably absent. In fact, my parents and Jeffrey weren't even home. I got the ritual crushing handshake from Grampa ("See ya soon, Muscles!"), let myself in, and staggered into the kitchen so I could consume heaping quantities of lifesaving meats and cheeses.

Or, in the case of our barren wasteland of a refrigerator, three-quarters of a thing of yogurt and half of a microwave bean burrito.

Then I booted up the computer so I could see how many people had e-mailed to check whether I was OK. I had seventeen new messages, which looked promising. But eleven were just spam — which would have been great if I had been seeking a cheaper mortgage or a way to "lose that weight fast!" I was looking for a bit of human contact and sympathy at the moment, so I went right to the six that were from actual people I knew, and they all said basically the same thing: "oh my god youve been absent for two (or three, or four) days and youre never absent. is jeffrey all right? hes in my prayers. We all miss u! ☹"

In case my friends' grammar and punctuation weren't upsetting enough, the fact that nobody thought there might be a problem with ME was enough to blacken my mood pretty thoroughly. I stormed over to the couch and called the one person who had gradually, without my even noticing it, become my confidante: Annette.

Hey. I'm home.

That's great! Are you all better? We really missed you in jazz band this week. And every teacher asked me about you. And some girl was pretty curious about where you were, too.

Who?

Oh, somebody.

Annette, I'm not in the mood to be tortured right now. Would ya just tell me, please?

I'm not sure about this, Steven. Your heart might not survive the strain of this if you're not fully recovered.

Annette . . .

OK, I'll give you a hint: She wears very tight shirts, and you drool over her like a deranged monkey boy.

WHAT? What are you TALKING about? I don't drool over Renee like a deranged anything.

But you knew who I meant right away, didn't you?

On the one hand, Renee continued to show remarkable, if sudden, interest in me. On the other hand, gggggrrrrrr! What was Annette's problem?

We talked for a while more, until she got called to dinner: veal parm. Evidently, there still existed an abundance of animal-based food if one knew where to find it. And if one were just too pathetic, forlorn, and unremembered, one could always scrounge up some decade-old, generic canned fruit cocktail from the depths of the basement pantry.

I was sitting at the kitchen table, alone, picking out the cherries from the various beige floaty things which made up 93% of the fruit cocktail, when my family returned home, laughing at some private joke that they had shared during my week in lockdown. Jeffrey looked at my parents for approval, and when my mom nodded, he launched himself into my lap.

I thought I'd never see you again.

Why? I just had the flu.

But Mommy said you were . . .

I know: dying. But I wasn't dying at all, and now I'm fine.

Then Mom piped up, *Oh, Stevie, it's great to have you back.*

Hey! You noticed I was gone? What was the big clue that gave it all away?

Steven AL-per! What has gotten into you?

The ensuing fight was not so entertaining for anyone concerned, although Jeffrey giggled when I said Grandma was a "demented child-starving hag."

Dad may have found some truth there, too, but he wasn't dumb enough to jump into the raging battle, so he just took Jeffrey off of the field of combat and up to bed. Without an audience, Mom and I wound down pretty fast, without any kind of resolution. I just kind of tapered off and walked away, went downstairs, and played on my practice pad. At first, my wrists were rusty after more than a week off, but I gradually warmed up until I was playing blazingly fast and much harder than usual. When I got too tired, I stopped for a while and listened to blasting punk music on my Discman. Then I went back to the pad again. I must have been down there, banging away, for a couple of hours — I was trying to stay hidden until everyone else went up to bed so I wouldn't have to deal with anybody. Finally, I decided the coast was probably clear, so I tiptoed upstairs.

Nobody was sleeping yet. As it turned out, my family hadn't necessarily been having the excellent week I had been imagining so resentfully. I could hear noises from the bathroom upstairs: Jeffrey vomiting and my mom trying to soothe him. I also saw something shocking — right in front of me, at the kitchen table, my dad was slumped over a pile of papers with his head cradled in his hands.

And he was crying.

POINTLESSNESS AND BOY PERFUME

If you had a father who hadn't shown any emotion for three or four months, and then you stumbled upon him weeping as though someone had just shot Bambi right in front of his eyes, what would you do? Right — you would sneak away and never let on that you had seen anything. And that's what I did. I crept back into the basement like a highly skilled sneak thief and then proceeded to listen to the most calming music I know: the Beatles. Somewhere between "Revolution" and "Hey, Jude" I fell asleep. When I awoke in a small puddle of my own drool on the ratty playroom carpet, with my left earphone seemingly welded to my head by the force of gravity, I looked at the Zildjian cymbal clock my parents once got me for a birthday. It was 11:45 p.m. I felt pretty sure of two things: Nobody had noticed that I was hidden away in the dark basement like a leper, and everybody would be asleep when I went upstairs this time. For a change, I was doubly right. In the kitchen,

I couldn't help but notice that my dad's mysterious pile of depressing papers was just sitting on the table, in plain view.

To see or not to see? That was the question. Well, for about a tenth of a second, anyway. Then I dove on those papers like Sherlock Holmes on a cappuccino binge. What I was looking at, what had turned my strong, silent dad into a weepy mass of pudding, was a stack of bills. Medical bills. Jeffrey's bills. The top sheet, which was written in my dad's handwriting, was a tally of the total unpaid amount to date: $27,000. The total expenses so far were unbelievable, definitely in the six-figure range. If not for the fact that my parents both had good health insurance (which I knew from overhearing some discussions about this stuff), we would already have blown the whole cost of a college education in these three months — and I knew Jeffrey was going to need at least three YEARS of treatment. As it was, I figured I'd be attending the University of "Would You Like Some Fries with That?" There was no way either of us would have any kind of college fund at the end of this. Then I had an even more depressing thought: Jeffrey might not be around long enough to go to college.

OK, so we were losing money hand over fist, my dad was crumbling like a day-old scone, and my brother might die. Really, what could I do about any of it? At the moment, the only answer I could come up with was "Nothing."

I went upstairs to get ready for bed, and a new obsessive slogan started running through my mind. It worked like this: "OK, I'll brush my teeth now. But Jeffrey might die, so what's the point? Time to wash my face. But Mom's not working, Dad makes maybe $40,000 a year after taxes, and there's $27,000 in unpaid bills downstairs. We're going to be homeless any minute — so what's the point? I should floss now, too, but I didn't even brush, so what's the point?" So I went to bed with a grimy face and yuck-encrusted teeth. And that was just the start of my depressing What's the Point? period.

The next day, I came back from my week of

absence to a barrage of "oh my god what's wrong with Jeffrey is your mom okay how's your dad taking it what you were sick oh." You can imagine that that didn't snap me out of my funk too well. Renee talked with me all through homeroom, which should have made me ecstatic, but I just kept thinking, "Soon I'll be leaving school to go live under an overpass, so what's the point of Renee liking me now?" Also, somewhere in the back of my mind I was realizing that she hadn't suddenly discovered that I was an actual human-being-type person because of any new attributes I had developed; she was just temporarily fascinated by me as a tragic figure. I still couldn't help going gaga over how beautiful she was, but I was almost mad at her, because she wasn't noticing me for the right reasons.

Annette was truly concerned about me, though. In Miss Palma's class, she offered to come over after school a few days that week and catch me up on my class work in every subject we had together. That was pretty comforting, because I didn't want to fail all of my finals after the massive makeup effort I had done before my flu episode, and Annette always got A's in everything.

There was one problem: My math period was Annette's piano period, so who would bail me out in math? I was tempted to say, "I'm going to fail the hardest subject anyhow, so what's the point?" I didn't, though — I was determined to pull all of my grades through this so I wouldn't add to my parents' worries. In math class, I went to the teacher and told him I would need help if I wanted to learn the week of new material I'd missed. I was torn between hoping he'd offer to meet me during our opportunity period and teach me the stuff himself and being afraid that spending that much time one-on-one with a math teacher would crack me completely and turn me into a deranged lunatic. "Oh, well," I figured, "at least I'll be the life of the under-bridge party crowd then."

The teacher did not offer to catch me up, though. Instead, he asked for a volunteer who was willing to tutor me at home. And he got one: Renee

Albert. Holy cow. Renee Albert was coming to my house! RENEE ALBERT WAS COMING TO MY HOUSE! Even *I* couldn't think, "What's the point of Renee Albert coming to my house?" with a straight face. I just said, "Wow, thanks, Renee!" while every other guy in the class looked at me like I had a big target painted on my forehead.

It was one of my drum lesson days with Mr. Watras, and when I walked in, he handed me a crumpled tissue, pointed to the garbage can, and told me to show him my newfound hoops skills. I got it in — swish! — and sat down at the drum set. It was a great feeling to be playing drums after more than a week away from them, and Mr. Watras must have understood because he just sat back and watched me burning around the kit at full speed for a couple of minutes. When I stopped, he surprised me by talking about my academic situation, which we had never discussed again after the ugly meeting I'd had with my teachers.

So, I hear you've made up all of your old work.
Yeah.

Do you have a plan for making up the work you missed last week and studying for finals?

Yes, Annette is going to tutor me in everything except math, and this, um, other girl is going to help me with the math.

Great! Listen, Steven, I'm really glad you're back on track with this school stuff. We absolutely depend on you in All-City, and I'm thrilled that we can keep you in the ensemble.

Me, too.

But part of me was thinking, "What's the point of practicing for a stupid concert when my brother might not live to see it?"

The week went by like that, with me going to school, my mom and Jeffrey coming and going between home and Philly, my dad staring off into space even more than he had been for months. I kept having those "What's the point of . . . ?" moments, but plugged away at life pretty consistently, anyway. And Annette came by three times to help me study.

You know what? She was an amazing tutor. I understood everything when she explained it, and got hundreds on a social studies quiz and a science lab thanks to her. There was an awkward moment when she first saw Jeffrey, because it was her first time seeing him all bald and puffy, but she covered her shock well. And by the second night, she was playing board games with him every time she took a break while I did practice quizzes or writing assignments. He was happy with the attention, and I noticed something interesting: She was much more patient and honestly excited to play with him than I was.

So Annette was the absolute perfect tutor pal, and I should have been kissing the ground beneath her feet and carrying her book bag to school every day, right? But even while I was getting so much from her, I couldn't stop thinking about next week, when Renee would be coming over.

On Thursday night of that week, Mom and Jeffrey left for a quick two-day trip to Philly for blood counts and a couple of chemotherapy injections. The procedures were pretty routine by then, but the results weren't. Jeffrey's counts were really low, so low that the doctors gave him two transfusions: one of whole blood and one of platelets. This turned the two-day trip into a four-day trip. I heard my dad on the phone saying that the hospital bills were running about $2,000 a night, so I knew our financial picture wasn't getting any rosier. Also, my mom told me that Jeffrey would probably be even more vulnerable to germs in the foreseeable future, so I should be extra-careful to avoid being near anyone who was sneezing or coughing, and to wash my hands when I walked into the house every day. I asked if I should just stay home and live in a plastic bubble with Jeffrey, and she warned me that I might, in fact, have to stay out of school for a while if something like chicken pox started going around.

So I was freaking out. On the one hand, my head was a mess of tumbling worries: rising poverty, falling blood counts, alarming potential for quarantine. On the other hand, Renee was coming! RENEE WAS COMING! To! My! HOUSE!

Tuesday was the big day. Midterm exams were a week away, so I needed Renee's help pretty big-time. Also, I couldn't get past the excitement part of the deal: Renee! In my house! I missed math for a drum-section rehearsal (you really have to love the logic of getting called out of math for band right before exams), and Renee wasn't on the bus on the way home from school. So we didn't confirm that she would be coming over, but I assumed the plan was on for 7:00 p.m., which was what we had arranged the week before.

I ate with my mom and Jeffrey at 6:00; my dad was still at his office. It was the beginning of tax season, when accountants get busier and busier leading up to April 15th. I figured we could use some extra income, so I was betting my dad would be really busy this year. Anyway, my mom noticed that I was being quieter than usual, and Jeffrey started in.

He's saving up all his smooth talking for his big date with Renee Albert.

It's not a date, nutball. She's just tutoring me in math.

I bet you're gonna kiss her, right?

She has a boyfriend, Jeffrey. You know that. She's still going out with Biff, the guitar player.

But she's coming over to play with you.

She's not playing with me; she's teaching me about numbers and stuff.

So when are you going to kiss her, then?

MOM! The kid is out of control. Can't we get him some tranquilizers or something? Maybe a padded cell upstairs?

Then my mom got rolling. *Steven, is there something going on between you and Renee? I notice you're dressed more neatly than usual, and your hair is even combed down.*

And he's wearing boy perfume, Mom. He wasn't wearing any last week when Annette came over, but for RENEE he is.

It's called cologne, monkey boy.

Since when do you wear cologne to learn math? Oh, my son is growing up right in front of my very eyes. Maybe I should get out the video camera.

Maybe you should tie me to a stake, douse me in kerosene, and torch me right on our front lawn.

I won't need any kerosene, Steven — I'm sure the cologne will go up pretty fast!

Ha-ha, Mom.

Just then the doorbell rang.

Please keep the lunatic away from us, Mom. We have work to do.

Is kissing hard work or easy work, Steven?

MOM! REMOVE HIM!

I went to answer the door, and when I opened it, Renee was standing there, all bundled up against the winter, with a few snow-flurry flakes on her jacket. Her cheeks were flushed from the wind, and her hair was blowing around. I just wanted to reach out and brush the strands away from her face, but that didn't seem like a good tutorial beginning, plus Biff looked like the kind of guy who could rip my arms off and use them as toothpicks. So I just said hi instead.

She said hello back, and I was just about to step aside and let her in. But just then, she sneezed. And coughed. And sneezed again.

Excuse me, Steven. I'm coming down with some kind of virus thingy, I think. I went home early from school today and skipped cheering, but I didn't want to stand you up. You have so many big problems going on, I just couldn't let you down. So I'm here. Let's get to work!

I blocked the doorway with my body and said something that seemed to float up from a place beyond my worst nightmares.

Renee, I can't let you in.

What do you mean? It's cold out here, and we've got a lot to do.

I mean, I'm sorry, but I can't let you come into this house. You're sick, and Jeffrey can't get sick right now.

Steven, you're being ridiculous. It's probably just a cold, anyway.

A cold could put my brother in the hospital.

Steven, what's really going on? Do you hate math so much you just can't stand it? Do you want to fail the class? Then I wish you would have told me that before I came stomping through the snow to come over here.

Renee, I'm serious. This isn't about math.

And it can't be about ME. Any boy in the school would be drooling to have me come over. And everybody knows you've had a crush on me since third grade, haven't you? Now just let me IN!

I'm sorry, Renee. Do you want me to call your mom to come get you?

Without responding to me directly, she spun around on her heels like the dancer she was and marched away. I could hear her muttering about me all the way to the end of the driveway:

Uuugggghhh! I walk to the boy's house in a BLIZ-ZARD, and he doesn't even let me IN. He drools over me for half a DECADE, but when I deliver myself to his front DOOR, he slams it in my FACE! I will NEVER underSTAND boys! At that point, she fired a parting shot over her shoulder. *Go ahead, then, fail math and be lonely the rest of your life.*

As I slumped against the door frame, staring at her back and wondering how she could be so grace-ful in snow boots and a parka when she wasn't even feeling well, Jeffrey came up behind me.

You know, Steven, you were right. I guess you aren't going to kiss her.

THE SILVER LINING

$\mathcal{OK}$, a quick status report, as of the end of January:

1. My family was plunging into poverty.

2. My brother had no immune system.

3. My mom had no job.

4. My dad was working about ninety hours a week and appeared to be on the verge of flipping out completely.

5. The hottest girl in the eighth grade came to my house to tutor me, and I booted her off of my property.

6. I was definitely going to fail my math final.

But on a brighter note, my strange, tragedy-induced popularity at school was growing. Word got around that Steven Alper was the guy who kicked Renee Albert to the curb, and people just decided I must be the MAN. Annette was especially thrilled with the whole story for some reason; maybe she figured she'd have no competition for Tutor of the Year now.

Of course, every male I knew thought that sending Renee home made me the Idiot Boy of East Village Middle School, but they still felt an odd sort of admiration for me. It was like I had resisted the spell of a fearsome enchantress — everyone else was under that spell and COULDN'T resist it, so they assumed I had some secret strength. It didn't matter that they were wrong, that every time Renee walked into homeroom and glared at me, I was torn between two equally powerful urges: to run up to her, drop to one knee, and propose or to run away from her and cry in the boys' bathroom for an hour. All they saw was a guy who sent the Cheer Queen packing.

Weird.

Annette met with me after school a bunch more times that last week, my brother and mom went to Philly and returned, I played drums and did homework, meals got nuked and consumed, the sun rose in the East and set in the West. Numbness was setting in, but I had just enough oomph left to get me through finals.

I wound up with As and Bs in English, science, social studies, and Spanish, and a big, fat D in math. Mrs. Galley called me into her office one Friday to break the news.

Candy heart, Steven?

Last time I had been there, I practically had to donate blood to get a candy heart. Now she was leading off by offering me one? That right there was enough to tell me she hadn't sent for me so she could award me an honor roll T-shirt.

What did I do wrong, Mrs. Galley? I made up every scrap of work in every class, I got a tutor, I studied like a monk . . .

You got a thirty-seven on your math final.

Huh, how 'bout that? I thought for sure I'd get at least a thirty-nine with that extra credit problem about the two trains.

Steven, I'm truly sorry. You made an incredible effort right up until the end.

Yeah, so did the dodo bird, the passenger pigeon, Vanilla Ice . . .

How are your parents going to take this news? I know you were quite concerned about their reaction when you had all that homework to make up.

Uh . . . I don't know, really. I've never gotten lower than a B+ before, but on the other hand, they're pretty caught up in my brother's situation right now. Maybe they just kinda won't notice?

I'm sorry to break it to you, Steven, but I have a feeling they'll notice this.

I know. How are they going to find out? Are report cards getting mailed home today, or will you call first, or will I have a chance to tell them?

Your report card is probably already in your mailbox. Do you want me to call them before they see it?

Yes, please. You can get my mom on her cell phone. She's at the hospital with Jeffrey today, but she always has it with her. Please tell her I tried. Please?

She said she would "certainly advocate" for me and then asked whether I wanted to be in the office for the call. I really and truly didn't want to sit there and watch the live action as my mom got disappointed in me, so I went back to class. I buried my head and got through the rest of the day, but the bus ride home felt like a condemned man's last walk.

Of course, when I got home, nobody was there. The answering machine had two messages: Dad would be home by 10 p.m., and I should eat without him (well, DUH!), and Mom and Jeffrey would be staying at the hospital another night, but I should call my mom's cell phone ASAP.

Now here was an interesting dilemma. Should I call and face the problem or not call and enjoy a few hours of lonely, nerve-wracking boredom, instead of my usual lonely, depressing boredom? I pondered that for about seven-tenths of a second before finally going downstairs to play drums until "dinner." While I was in the basement playing, it occurred to me that my mom might worry when she didn't hear back, but I just wasn't in the mood to consider somebody else's feelings at the moment.

Unfortunately, it also didn't occur to me that my mom might completely spaz and send my dad home to check on me. Imagine my surprise when basement lights went out! I stopped playing, took off my headphones, and jumped up. The lights went back on. When my eyes re-adjusted, I was looking straight into the vengeful glare of an enraged accountant.

Steven! It's 6:30. What are you doing?

Ummm . . . playing drums?

Why didn't you call your mother when you got home?

Why should I have? She's just going to yell at me for my math grade, right?

You should have called her because when you DIDN'T, she was afraid you'd disappeared or something. So she had me paged out of an important meeting, and I came charging home. This cost us about $200 . . . and we don't HAVE $200. It was irresponsible, Steven.

Ooohhhh, irresponsible. That's, like, the dirtiest word an accountant can possibly say to his kid. I knew things were at a crucial point right now: What I said next would likely determine whether I'd be grounded until marriage or just lectured for a while and then ignored again. But every once in a while, you don't make the safest choice when you're thirteen.

IRRESPONSIBLE? Irresponsible, Dad? You really want to talk about "irresponsible?" I don't THINK you do! Who's the super-responsible guy who hasn't actually talked to his firstborn son about ANYTHING in about four months? Who's the pillar of reliability who has left his thirteen-year-old to fend for himself for weeks on end? When was the last time you asked me about school, RESPONSIBLE MAN? When was the last time you went shopping for any food that can't be cooked using two minutes of radiation?

Steven, that's not fair.

FAIR? You banished me to the old folks' home for a week, and you want to talk to me about "fair"?

Steven, you know we had to take care of your brother.

Now I was in full-on attack formation. It was like I was playing some kind of Dad Devastator III video game or something — I just couldn't stop saying the coldest, meanest things that popped into my head.

WHO had to take care of my brother? Have you

168

been playing board games with him every night instead of studying for school? Have you been kneeling with him in front of the toilet every time he throws up? Have you been sleeping at the hospital with him? Have you . . .

I stopped for a moment and looked up at my father; truthfully, I was kind of surprised he hadn't smacked me yet. What I saw wasn't quite what I would have expected. He had sat down heavily on the basement steps, and his head was bowed. He looked like a dog does right after you whack it with a newspaper.

Ummm, Dad? Dad?

His voice was a hollow whisper that I hadn't heard before and hoped I'd never hear again. *You're right, Steven. You're 100% right. I have not been talking with you, and I haven't been taking care of anybody. I haven't been . . . I haven't . . . since your brother's . . . since October . . .*

This was the longest string of words he had uttered in months, but it suddenly dried up, as if he just couldn't find any more to say. And then he looked at me with this tenderness that was also totally new to me, stood up, and held his arms open.

I know this sounds weird, right in the middle of a fight and all, but I ran right into my dad's chest. After he held me for a while, I tried to speak. *Dad, I don't want Jeffrey to* . . .

Then I cried until it was time for embarrassment, burritos, and a long call from Dad to Mom.

When my father hung up, he looked much more like my old dad, my pre-October dad. He was still kind of talked-out, but there was one more thing on his accountant brain.

So about that math grade . . .

The next day, Mom and Jeffrey came home. When they walked in, they encountered a scene that must have been fairly surprising: My dad and I were playing chess at the kitchen table, and there was a pile of my math stuff on one of the extra chairs. Dad had spent a couple of hours that morning getting me two chapters ahead in algebra. After I had explained the whole Renee Albert tutorial fiasco, he had felt sorry for his pathetic eldest boy. You sometimes forget how good your parents are at things. I mean, my dad did math for a living, 365 days a year, so it made sense that he knew the stuff. But, I mean, he REALLY knew the stuff. Then when we were done, we celebrated with my first cup of coffee ever and the chess game. (Weird. My parents would NEVER have let me have coffee before Jeffrey got sick. If there's one thing I'd figured out about having a family crisis like ours, it's that the old rules no longer applied — for example, I had probably gone four months without eating a single vegetable. But there were times when I wished for new rules that DID apply — like maybe, "Take a vitamin every day so you don't get scurvy.") I got all hyped-up from the caffeine and won the game in about nine minutes, so my father got a chance to be impressed by ME, too.

And then when my mom and Jeffrey sat down at the table, it was like some kind of normal family moment or something. Until my mom remembered she was mad at me. She asked my dad to take Jeffrey into the living room for some father-son bonding (ol' Dad was having quite the paternal morning) and then began lacing into me. But before she could build up a good head of steam, I cut her off and explained how hard I had worked on the grades, how disappointed I was in myself, how I had turned away the world's most desirable math tutor for the sake of Jeffrey's health, and how my dad and I had already had it out about the "not calling Mom's cell phone" incident.

What could she really say?

Steven, I love you. But never, ever do this again.

There. I could live with that.

The rest of the weekend was pretty tranquil for a change. Jeffrey was on a new antinausea medication, and the doctors had lowered his steroid dose, so he was feeling well enough to play more actively. Also, thanks to my little math mini-drama, both parents were looking right at me and even asking me questions about my life. Probably the coolest part was my drum lesson with Mr. Stoll on Saturday afternoon. My mom drove me instead of sleeping, which was her usual post-hospital routine, and watched the whole lesson instead of going shopping or something.

Afterward, she told me she'd had no idea how good I had gotten. It felt pretty nice to know that my last four months of being a practice-pad maniac had made a noticeable difference. As things turned out, it was a good thing my mom had watched that particular drum lesson, because it would be the last one we'd be able to afford for a long while.

On Sunday, my cousins from New York City came over, which they hadn't done in ages — my mom had called them when she noticed that Jeffrey was suddenly having a couple of good days, and her sister had dropped everything to come see us while the opportunity lasted. I'm the oldest kid in our whole extended family, so I generally run around keeping the little ones from killing each other, but that day they all got along. I sat on our back porch, drinking hot chocolate, thinking about Renee Albert, and watching my brother and the cousins pound each other with snowballs for about forty minutes — an endurance record for Jeffrey this year.

When they came in, we had a real family-style dinner — my mom had even dusted off that big thing in the kitchen called the "stove" — and people were laughing and joking around like we used to last year. I mean, an outside observer would notice that there was a puffy, bald kid there and that the grown-ups kept pausing to look furtively at him, but the mood was lighter than it had been since the diagnosis, anyway. Jeffrey even got my uncle Neil to do his famous impression of Peter Pan and Captain Hook fighting over dessert, which he only did once a year. It was a really nice time.

Then Jeffrey started falling asleep at the table; I guess all that running around had been tough on his body. The adults were all taking their time over coffee, and the cousins were in the family room watching *SpongeBob,* so I took Jeffrey up to bed. Even though he was only half-awake, I got him to go pee-pee and brush his teeth. Then we went into his room to get his PJs on. He took off his shirt and I gasped: His arms were an alarming welter of dark bruises. I hadn't thought of it at the time, but I guess all of the snowballs hitting him had taken a toll, even through his thick winter coat. He glanced up at me with this look of total resignation that should never be on a five-year-old face. I felt so bad for him that I read him two chapters of his favorite book, *Flat Stanley*, before I turned off his light.

Later on, after the guests had left, I said good night to my parents and got ready to go to bed myself. I had been in a nearly great mood for about thirty-six hours but unease was settling back in. When I was lying down all alone in the dark, I couldn't get comfortable for the longest time. I just kept seeing Jeffrey's arms over and over in my head, and it hit me: I had been in a dreamworld for a day and a half. But just because you get distracted by the silver lining for a little while, that doesn't mean there's not still a huge dark cloud behind it.

FEAR, GUM, CANDY

That night, I started having the Dream. I was playing outside with Jeffrey, and we were throwing something back and forth (sometimes a tennis ball, sometimes a snowball). Every time the ball touched Jeffrey, a piece of him would instantly turn black. He was still smiling and saying, *Play with me, play with me!* every time I tried to stop. So I'd throw again, and BAM! Again, BAM! Again, BAM! Then he'd slowly start sinking into the ground, still with that smile on his face, as my parents appeared behind him. And he'd start saying over and over again, *You're their only boy. You're their only son. You're the only boy now.* And I'd wake up screaming at the top of my lungs. I had the Dream — with slight variations — maybe every other night for the next two months. Thankfully, Jeffrey somehow always slept through it. My parents didn't, though; they eventually got so used to it happening that they started getting to my bed and grabbing me before I even woke myself up. Every time this happened, they would ask me what the

Dream was about, and every time, I'd lie and say I didn't remember.

My parents started pressuring me to tell Mrs. Galley about the Dream, which I just didn't want to do. I thought, "Why would I need to tell her? What's she going to do — send me to a psychiatrist? I'm not crazy — I'm having dreams that my extremely ill brother is dying, which makes sense!" I hated the dreams with a burning passion, but the fact that I was having them didn't seem like a big blockbuster of a surprise to me.

So for the time being, my parents' worries about their younger son's physical health were compounded by their worries about their older son's mental health. My dad paced back and forth a lot when he was home, my mom asked me a thousand times a day how I was doing, and I basically just pretended it was totally normal to wake up drenched with sweat, shrieking like a wounded banshee, night after night. In the meantime, my mom was also asking for advice about this from all of the doctors, nurses, social workers, and assorted therapy-type people in the Philly hospital, and every single one of them told her to get me into counseling as soon as she could. Some helpful soul down there also told her that "experiencing" Jeffrey's treatment "firsthand" by visiting the hospital might "alleviate" my "anxiety."

So she started bugging me to come down to Philly on one of the weekly trips, but every time she asked, I had an excuse handy: jazz band rehearsal. Schoolwork. Drum lesson. Anything to keep me away from the mental-health providers. Sure, I was plagued by nightmares. Absolutely, I was tormented by repeated bouts of What's the Point? Syndrome. And there was no question that I was terrified by everything about Jeffrey's treatment.

But I was coping, right? I was getting good grades in the third marking period, I was still improving rapidly on drums, I continued to be oddly popular at school. I had even patched things up with Renee Albert. One day on the bus, she caught me looking at her and stared back. Thinking fast, I made her an irresistible offer.

Gum?

You're offering me gum? Really?

Yeah, really.

Aren't you afraid I'll try to contaminate it?

Well, it's only going into your own mouth, so feel free.

I noticed that there were about twelve people watching this scene — like it was a jury trial or something — so I scooted across the aisle to sit by Renee and continue the peace talks in whatever privacy you can have on a packed school bus chugging along a main thoroughfare.

Come on, Renee. Are you really going to be mad at me because I protected my baby brother by sending you home?

Well . . .

I failed the math final if it's any consolation.

You did? I'm sorry. Did your parents flip?

Kinda. Don't worry about it — it was my own fault I tuned out of that class for two months.

No, Steven, you had a lot on your mind. I'm sorry I got mad at you, and I'm sorry about the things I said.

Well, you were right. I did have a crush on you in third grade.

Do you have a crush on me now?

She gave me the killer Renee Albert smile and took the piece of gum from my instantly sweaty palm.

Just then, the bus pulled up to our stop. I reached back and across the aisle to get my backpack, and Annette held it out to me, glaring like I had been chatting with Renee about Annette's mother or something. I didn't have time to figure that one out; we weren't blessed with the most patient bus driver on the planet. I charged up to the front and out the door. The driver was already slamming down on the gas pedal while I was in midair, so I didn't turn around in time to catch Annette's eye through the window. I wondered whether she'd still be mad the next day and why I never seemed to be able to be friends with more than one human female at a time. When I got my bearings, I realized Renee was already walking away from me toward her house. For some odd reason — perhaps my brain had just reached its Female Logic Overload Point — I didn't call out after her.

As she turned the corner, without ever looking back to be sure I was still there staring, she said something to me, and I could hear the laughter in her voice. *Thanks for the gum!*

I kept looking until she was out of sight behind the huge, old oak tree at the end of the block. Boy, did that girl know how to walk.

So I was hanging in there. But the weirdness of acting "normal" when nothing really was normal was exhausting. One day, I fell asleep in social studies class, and the teacher took me out into the hall to talk about it.

How are you, Steven? Is there more bad news at home?

(No, things are just swell! We spend our time knitting matching sweaters, baking wholesome cookies from scratch, and watching my brother's hair fall out. Moron.)

No, I just have, ummm, a lot on my mind. Can I . . . Think fast, Steven! . . . *go see the school counselor?*

Of course, he let me go; I had already figured out that most teachers did NOT want to stand in the corridor talking about pediatric cancer when they could be safely in their rooms, handing out worksheets.

Mrs. Galley looked happy to see me, which was a nice feeling. Maybe I had only asked to see her so I could get out of class, and maybe I was merely in the mood for a candy heart or two, but I really was starting to trust this woman. She asked me how things had gone with the Math Grade Bust Weekend and in the weeks of school since then. I told her the whole story of that first weekend with my parents, and about how I was keeping up with my work and social life. She looked relieved that my 'rents hadn't tied me to a stump behind the woodshed and given me a beating. And I could have left it at that, with Mrs. Galley feeling like she had done a successful good deed by letting me choose how to handle my makeup work and my mom's notification, and with me feeling like I had earned some cinnamon-flavored snackage . . . but it wasn't the whole story.

Mrs. Galley, I can't sleep at night. I have this nightmare over and over again. I'm playing catch with my brother, and . . . I paused, and she quickly slid a box of tissues over to me. See, this lady was good!

I talked for another half-period, at least, and didn't stop until that tissue box was looking pretty undersupplied. She listened and listened and even turned off her incoming phone line. About five different people stuck their heads into her office, but she shooed them all away and finally locked her door. Every once in a while, she asked a question or two, but she basically just let me rip. At the very end, I summed up by telling her how out of control I felt — like I couldn't affect any of the problems that were all around me.

I can't wave a wand and make Jeffrey better. I can't call my Swiss banker and have him wire-transfer a couple million dollars to my parents' account. I can't even make my family FEEL better about anything. All I do is sulk, cry, and yell at my parents.

But you DO make your family feel better. I know Jeffrey must appreciate all of the playtime you spend with him, and I could tell when I talked to your mother that she was very proud of how responsible you have been. Sending away your math tutor — that took real courage.

You have no idea, Mrs. G.

Yeah, but I can't change all the ROOTS of the problems. I can't change the basic situation.

Well, Steven, I have to send you back to class now, because I have a group of students coming in. But I want to leave you with one thing to think about: Instead of agonizing about the things you can't change, why don't you try working on the things you CAN change?

I thanked her and took a candy heart (OK, a few) for the road. And a couple of tissues. And I made her promise she'd call me back down the next week. While I was on a roll, maybe I should have asked her to stock up on some new desk candy, too, but there are times when you just don't push your luck.

Over the next few days, my head was a jumble of battling quote bubbles.

ME: "What's the point of . . . ?"

MRS. GALLEY: "Why don't you try working on the things you CAN change?"

Of course, that was when I was awake. When I was asleep, the nightmares just kept on coming. I was starting to wonder whether I was going to be a nervous wreck for years and years, finally losing it completely and waking up in a mental ward with a tight, white sleeveless coat on.

Then, two things happened in quick succession. I figured out how to save some money, and Annette fell down a flight of stairs.

GOOD NEWS, BAD NEWS

If you think about it, past a certain point, drum lessons are a complete waste of money. You go there, and some guy listens to you playing a couple of book exercises and jamming to a few CDs. Then he assigns you new book exercises and CDs, and your mom pays him $20 for the hour. Next, you repeat as necessary for a bunch of years. So I realized one day that — hey! — I had all the drum books and CDs I could ever need, and I could assign myself the next two pages of each book every week. All I had to do was bag my drum lessons, and I'd be saving the family eighty bucks a month.

Just like Mrs. Galley said: *Why don't you try working on the things you CAN change?*

But how do you tell this to your drum teacher after five years together? This wasn't just any old drum teacher, either. Mr. Stoll had attended every single one of my school concerts since I'd started lessons. He had invited me to probably ten of his gigs to watch him play and had once let me sit in on drums at a big band concert for a thousand people. At the time, I had just been terrified, but later, I figured out how amazingly cool that had been of him.

So I couldn't just stop showing up. I needed a grand gesture to soften the blow, and I came up with a beautiful one. The day of the last lesson came, and I asked my mom to drop me off a few minutes early and to let me pay Mr. Stoll, then meet her outside at the end — I hadn't told the 'rents anything about this plan and didn't want to take any chances of Mom and Mr. Stoll talking that day. I had shoved something into my stick bag before leaving the house and was all ready for action.

So I went in, we exchanged pleasantries, and I even got through a few exercises before Mr. Stoll noticed I was all sweaty and shaky.

What's wrong, kid?

Well, uhhh, I have some bad news.

What, did you get kicked out of All-City or something?

Worse.

Is it about your brother?

Not exactly. I . . . we . . . my family has a lot of expenses with the hospital thing, and my parents are all worried about money, and I decided . . . I can't have drum lessons anymore. I'm sorry, but we can't afford it, and I can't pay, and I'm sorry.

You said that already, kid.

I did? I'm sorry.

There ya go again.

I, well, I brought you something. Let me just get it.

I reached into my bag and pulled out Mr. Stoll's gift. I kept it behind my back for a moment, then said, *Look, you've really been like a . . . ummm . . . like a mentor to me, and you've taught me more than I could ever have imagined, and I wanted to give you something to remember me by. So, anyway, here it is.*

And I held the Special Sticks out to him. You remember, the ones that Carter Beauford of the Dave Matthews Band, my drumming idol, signed for me? The ones Jeffrey used to stir his Dangerous Pie?

Kid, those are your prized possession. Taking those would be like kicking you when you're down. Listen, how about we just . . . look, from now on, your lessons are free. Don't worry about it. It's my pleasure to help my best student out.

Really? You REALLY mean it?

Yeah, I do. Now, let's get back to work. We were on page seventeen of the rudiment book, right?

Yes, SIR!

Oh, one other thing. Ya might want to spray those things with Lysol or something. Is it me, or do they smell like rotten eggs?

At the end of the lesson, I realized that I couldn't tell my mom that I had made this deal with Mr. Stoll, so I just ripped up the check she had given me. I knew that in the long run, that was about as useful as duct-taping over your car's fuel gauge so you won't run out of gas. But in the short run, delusion was an easier path than truth. And come on — you have to admit the deception was all for a good cause.

That week after school, we were supposed to be having rhythm-section rehearsal for All-City on Tuesday and Thursday. Our concert was only a month away, and we needed the extra tightening-up work. On Tuesday, Annette was absent, so I was the only one in our van on the way to the high school. I walked into the high school band room and started setting up the conga drums next to the drum set. Renee's boyfriend, Biff, was already plugging in his guitar, the bass player was tuning up, and the senior pianist was warming up with scales. After the usual round of "Hi, Pez," "Hi, Pez," "Hi, Pez," everyone turned toward the band room door, which was slowly creaking open. Biff called out, *You can come in. It's OK — the Peasant is fully housebroken. He almost never bites anymore.*

An arm came through the space between the door and the frame. An arm encased in a cast. Annette's arm. Then we heard her voice: *A little help here? Anybody?*

The bass player was closest, so he went trotting over and opened the door all the way. Annette came staggering in; she had been trying to carry a huge folder of sheet music in the crook of her injured arm. As Mr. Watras saw what was going on, he walked over, too, just in time to hear Annette's tale.

Here's my folder; I won't be playing in the spring concert. I fell down the stairs at my house last night an broke my arm in three places. They said it won't be better until at least May. I'm sorry.

Mr. Watras looked pretty perturbed by this news — every teacher in the world has a soft spot for Annette, plus the girl's a musical dynamo. He was very kind about it, though.

It's OK, Annette. Why don't you come on in, make yourself comfortable, and stay for the rehearsal? You can be our critic. Would you dig that? (Yes, he *was* the last man in America who could say "dig" with a straight face without referring to the process of using a tool to remove dirt from the ground.)

She didn't look like this was the chance of a lifetime or anything, but she did smile a little then. I had a feeling she would have been crushed to be excluded completely, and this gave her a way to stick around and still feel like she belonged.

Sure. Thanks, Mr. W.

We settled down for practice. It must have been

hard for Annette, but she watched us play for the next two hours without a break. Occasionally, she'd whisper something to the senior piano player or Mr. Watras, but other than that, all she did was listen and listen to the music she wouldn't be able to play.

I, on the other hand, was on *fire* that day. When I was playing the set, all four limbs just knew what to do without my even having to think. In fact, the less I thought, the better I played. There was this one part of a tune called "Satin Doll" where the band stopped dead and I had a gigantic fill that I typically screwed up at least once per rehearsal. I had tried everything: counting, having Mr. W. conduct me through it, NOT counting, closing my eyes, reading the music, ignoring the music. Things just hadn't clicked. But that day, I didn't even blink an eye; the other instruments dropped out and the next thing I knew, they came back in. I hadn't even noticed I was playing the solo-break part, but I must have nailed it, because Mr. W. was smiling and Annette gave me a little approving nod. It was like one of the Zen-master moments in a movie when the master suddenly figures out the secret of the universe without trying. Well, OK, it was a LITTLE Zen-master moment, like maybe when the master figures out the secret of Phillipsburg, New Jersey. It was still cool, though.

I was so far into the Zone that even Renee's arrival in her lycra uniform couldn't throw me off. In fact, for the first time in my life, I didn't even particularly pay attention to Renee — I was just having too much fun playing. The last thing we practiced was the big show finale, "Cubana Be, Cubana Bop." I got ready behind the congas, Brian shifted the drums around a bit so they'd be comfortable for him — he's about a foot taller than me — and Mr. W. and Annette came over. They were both going to do the chanting parts that were usually handled by the sax-ophone section, and Mr. W. was going to play the screaming trumpet parts, too. This piece had been pretty rough in practice so far, but some days, you just click — we were supertight through the whole tune. Brian was playing the kit so well that I felt like we were telepathic; it was as if my right hand and his right foot were wired to one brain. The bass player was locked in there also, so every walking quarter note he played was pulsing in exact time with Brian's left foot hi-hat clicks. Meanwhile, Biff played an astounding solo — the notes just seemed to shimmer in the air like floating fire — and Mr. W. was simply incredible. The piano player didn't know this part as well as Annette did — even though he usually played more than half of the show, this one was rightfully hers — but he rose to the occasion, too. At the end, we all just stopped and looked around with these massive, dumb-looking grins on our faces. Then Renee started clapping, and Mr. W. joined in. Maybe Annette would have clapped, too, if not for the cast, but from the pained look behind her smile, I wasn't too sure.

On the way home in the van, Annette told me the whole arm story. Then she asked how Jeffrey was doing, which I thought was amazing — here she was, with a limb all mangled and her piano career slammed into reverse gear, worrying about my brother. I swear, sometimes I just really felt like pinning a medal on that girl. Anyway, I told her about the whole money situation, and even about how I had tried to quit drum lessons. She looked impressed that I had been willing to sacrifice my lessons, and thought it was hilarious that the Special Sticks still smelled weird. Naturally, being Annette, she did feel the need to warn me about how ripping up my mom's checks wasn't going to work forever, but somewhere in the preceding half year, I had figured out that the lectures were just an Annette thing. In fact, I would nearly have been disappointed if she hadn't given me the big, fiery speech at that point. When we got to my house, we said a sad little good-bye, but I felt cheerful, in a way. Evidently, you could shatter Annette's arm, but you couldn't break her spirit.

CLOSE SHAVES IN AN UNFAIR WORLD

Here's a journal entry I wrote in English class the week of Annette's accident. It was actually on topic, which would have been a nice change of pace for Miss Palma — if I had let her read it. The assignment was "If you could pick one word in the English language to describe the universe, what would it be? Why?"

Here's my response:

Unfair.

Unfair.

Unfair, unfair, unfair.

What do you call a planet where bad guys stroll through life with success draped around their shoulders like a king's cloak, while random horrors are visited upon the innocent heads of children? I call it Earth.

You want examples? Just this week, my friend Annette (over there in the third row, by the way) was voluntarily taking groceries downstairs to her basement pantry. Now that right there is a meritorious feat — most of my friends stopped doing volunteer household chores in about fourth grade. But wait, there's more! She went to step down the first stair and realized her cat was snuggled up there. Rather than trample on the innocent feline, Annette attempted to do a little leap over said animal, while balancing about forty-seven cans of cat food in her arms. Now, this girl has a lot of God-given talents, but the grace of a ballerina is not one of 'em. So she lost her footing and tumbled down the steps amid a clanking metallic hail of small cans. And when her parents responded to her pitiful yelps of pain, (a) her mom stepped right on that darn cat, anyway, and (b) they found Annette's crumpled form at the foot of the stairs, head stuck to a pile of shopping bags by static cling, right arm twisted unnaturally into some sort of mathematically improbable three-dimensional rhombus shape. And Annette's right hand is pretty important, because the girl is a piano prodigy. OK, WAS a piano prodigy. Thanks, God.

But wait, there's STILL more. My little brother, Jeffrey — you know, the one that used to be a happy, healthy, normal kid until he was struck out of the blue by cancer — was making a semi-rare appearance in his kindergarten class yesterday. He's been absent quite a bit this year, what with the constant trips to the hospital to try and save his life and the total shutdown of his immune system and the frequent bouts of high fever and all. Anyhow, a new kid moved into the class, and he didn't know about Jeffrey's condition. So Jeffrey went up to him and said, "Hi. I'm Jeffrey. I'm five. Are you five? My brother is thirteen. Do you want to be friends?" And the new guy replied, "Hi, I'm Adam. You're bald."

I know it sounds weird. Jeffrey has certainly noticed the total lack of hair coverage on his head. But hearing it from another kid devastated him. Evidently, he had thought other people somehow couldn't tell he was bald or something. Whatever. When this one kid said, "You're bald," Jeffrey just burst out crying. He barely spoke all night at home, and at about 10 p.m., two hours after his bedtime, I walked by his bedroom and heard him sobbing in his bed. I asked him what was wrong, and he told me about the incident at school. Then I asked him why he hadn't told us earlier what was wrong, and he said the saddest thing: "I didn't want you to find out I was bald, too."

So now my baby brother who has leukemia has the added curse of self-conscious humiliation, too.

Unfair, unfair, unfair. Really, if that were the only word in the English language, the only word in all the world, the sum and total of all human expression across the long millennia, it would essentially cover all the bases. Everything else we say is pretty much irrelevant.

• • •

Maybe if Miss Palma had been allowed to read the journal entry, she would have understood why I shaved my entire head the next night. I was standing in the bathroom, getting ready for bed, and this little Gap Kids baseball hat was sitting on the ledge by the sink. I was thinking about how Jeffrey had worn the hat everywhere he went that day. And I was wondering whether he'd be keeping it on his head

every minute for months, just because of one innocent comment some kid had made. And I was
thinking, "Who cares whether the little rug rat
meant to hurt Jeffrey? He did, and now there's no
way to take it back." But then I heard Mrs. Galley's
voice saying, "Instead of agonizing about the things
you can't change, why don't you try working on
the things you *can* change?" And I realized that no, I
couldn't grow Jeffrey's hair back overnight like he
was some kind of mammalian Chia Pet, and no, I
couldn't retroactively sew shut the mouth of the
new kid who had unintentionally broken the news to
my brother. But I could show support for Jeffrey.
I could be bald, too.

I took out my dad's electric clipper and buzzed
off my whole head of hair to shorter and shorter
lengths until I thought it would be easy to shave with
an electric razor. Then I started in on the actual
shaving portion of the festivities. Now, OK, I've never
even shaved my face before, so perhaps I should have
figured out this wouldn't be a quick or painless
procedure. But the same inexperience that made me

cocky also made me unskilled. And it hurts using an electric razor on your head hair! Every few seconds, the razor would either get jammed with hair and need to be cleaned out or catch a chunk of hair and rip it out of my scalp.

When I was about three-quarters of the way done with my gruesome task of charitable self-mutilation, my mother barged into the bathroom.

I heard a strange buzzing noise in here. What are you . . . OH! Steven!!!

Surprise! I'm running away to become a Buddhist monk. You like the do?

Steven Richard Alper! What are you DOING?

I just told you: I'm . . .

Steven, SHUT UP!

Holy cow. Now THERE'S something you don't hear every day at our house.

You are going to tell me the truth RIGHT NOW. Do you understand me? I'm tired. We're all tired. We can't be putting up with any of your teenage . . .

I did this for Jeffrey, Mom. So he wouldn't have to be bald alone.

Oh, Stevie.

All of a sudden, Mom understood; I think she was probably even impressed. She stepped through the mounds of hair all over the bathroom tiles and put her arms around me for a long, long time. Then she pushed back from me, held me at arm's length, and turned me around, like I was a side of beef and she was a chef sizing me up for a barbecue.

Give me the razor. I'll finish this job. If I'm going to have two bald sons, at least they'll both be PRESENTABLE-looking bald sons.

In the morning, I went down to breakfast with a baseball cap on. My whole family was already down there, which was not the norm — but my mom had rushed everyone down so I could make a grand entrance, and I had dragged my feet for the same reason. I poured myself a bowl of delightfully sugar-encrusted cereal, and sat down at the table. I could tell from the look on my dad's face that he knew the deal and was dying to see my newly cleared scalp. Jeffrey had no clue, of course, and didn't even look up from his toaster pastry and juice. After a few minutes during which the only sounds were our little mini-symphony of slurping and crunching, I guess my dad couldn't take the suspense anymore. He told me to "Take off that hat at the table, young man." So, just as Jeffrey looked up — there's nothing he enjoys more than watching me get a good lecture — I whipped off the cap. I wish you could have seen his face. It went from puzzlement to alarm to puzzlement, and then finally to a shy little grin.

What do you think, Jeff? I did it last night after you were in bed. You look so handsome this way, I thought I could get the Jeffrey look, too. Do you think maybe now all the babes will love me the way they love you?

Jeffrey's smile got larger and larger, until it was as big as Christmas. He jumped up and hugged me. Then he pushed away, looked at me appraisingly for a long time. When he finally switched off the X-ray eyes, he said very solemnly, *I don't know, Steven. You look OK, I guess. But it will take more than just a haircut to turn you into a handsome babe magnet like me.*

Honestly, where does the child GET this stuff?

At school, my plan was to do the "hat trick" again until some teacher made me take the cap off. That would have been a swell strategy, too, if it hadn't been the windiest day of the whole year. As I was standing at the bus stop with Renee, a massive gust whipped that sucker right off my head and down the sidewalk. I'm sure I have looked more suave at other moments than I did right then, running up the street in a crouch, trying to jump on the flying headgear while carrying all my books, my pate shining in the glare of the strong morning sun. I finally got the hat pinned under my foot and looked up in momentary triumph — just as the bus pulled up.

Well, at least I finally stole the show from Renee Albert for a minute. I was the talk of the bus. Annette wasn't on board — it turned out she was late because of an orthopedist appointment — so I sat next to Renee.

She looked at me in an awed kind of silence usually only seen on three-year-olds who are meeting

Barney for the first time. Then she shook her head, as if to clear it, and spoke.

Wow, you must really love your brother.

Nah, I just really hate my hair. OK, once in a rare while, I *do* come up with a decent line under pressure!

When I got to school, word raced around the building, and I was like king of the island for a day. A couple of my friends thought I was nuts, but everyone else, especially girls and female teachers, thought I was . . . ummm . . . "soooooo sweet!"

I was pretty pleased with the outcome, overall, although I did have a complaint: The top of my head was freezing.

THE QUADRUPLE UH-OH

$\mathcal{A}$ couple of days later, at All-City rehearsal, Mr. Watras made a startling announcement to the group: The school district had just put a new policy in place. Evidently, every high school student would now have to perform community-service hours every semester in order to graduate, effective immediately. Everybody around me started mumbling and grumbling right away, but I didn't see what the big deal was. I asked Brian.

Well, Pez, here's the problem: A lot of us are already busy every day after school and Saturdays with this, our regular school bands, sports, jobs, relationships, and just generally trying to have a life and get decent grades. So . . .

Yeah?

So, some of us may have to drop out of All-City in order to do the service hours. That's the "big deal."

Oh.

About an hour into the rehearsal, I noticed that Annette and Renee were in their usual spots, watching the proceedings. But they weren't just watching — they were whispering back and forth at top speed. Now you know I don't know much about the inner workings of girl-folk — but I did realize that anything that could bring those two together had to have some pretty powerful voodoo to it.

By the time we were done playing, Annette and Renee were writing frantically. And not just notes. They were writing paragraphs, lists, charts, and graphs. Annette had a calculator; Renee was wielding — I swear to God — a compass (or possibly a protractor. I never could remember which is which). It was like they were planning a space mission or something.

The band stopped, and Annette strode over to the podium. She grabbed Mr. Watras's conducting baton and tapped it on the music stand just like he always does. Everyone looked over, and Annette started talking.

How many of you are going to have trouble meeting the service requirement and staying in All-City? Come on, raise your hands.

About three-quarters of the band did.

Wouldn't it be great if you could somehow get service credit for BEING in All-City?

People were looking interested now.

Because I think that Renee over there (Renee waved) and I have a way. Listen, guys. I'm sure you all know that there are families in this town who have dire financial situations, families that are trying their hardest but just can't seem to make ends meet, families that could use a helping hand. Am I right?

Well, sure she was right. But on the other hand, she was also starting to sound like a street-corner preacher. I, myself, felt vaguely like jumping up and shouting "AMEN!" but I figured it might be wise to find out what I would be "Amen"-ing about first.

Gentlemen of the All-City Jazz Band, we have an opportunity here to reach out that helping hand to one of our own. I know you are all aware of the serious health problems that Steven Alper's brother has had this year.

Oh, God.

But what you probably don't know is that little

Jeffrey's disease, leukemia, is tremendously expensive. The Alper family is struggling to pay their bills. Steven's mother has had to take a leave of absence from her job to take care of Jeffrey, so just when their need is greatest, half of their cash flow is gone.

Annette stopped for a moment, and Biff spoke into the silence.

Yeah, we all know about the Peasant's brother. What does that have to do with getting the band out of the service requirement?

It doesn't have to do with getting you out of the requirement. It has to do with getting the requirement into the band.

Huh?

We can make our concert a benefit for Steven's family. Renee, can you tell these guys about the numbers?

Hi, guys. We did some math here, and this could really work. If we charge $15 a ticket, and there are a thousand seats in the auditorium here, that's fifteen thousand right there. Then we have a bake sale set up in the lobby. Brian, don't your parents own a bakery?

Uhhh, yeah.

Maybe they could donate the stuff or sell it to us at cost. Anyway, I bet we could easily sell five hundred pastries, or whatever, at a dollar each, so that brings us to fifteen-five. Then there's the program. We could probably get a printer to donate or work at cost, too. Then we sell ad space. What's the going rate for yearbook pages? Three-fifty a page? If we got fifteen full pages of ads, that would be . . . uh, where is it? Oh, yeah, that would be another $5,250, for a total of $20,750! What do you think, guys?

Yeah! Woo-hoo! Save the Peasant family!

Personally, I thought my parents were either going to kiss the ground or wring my neck, and I had no idea which.

Before everybody left, Annette and Renee got Mr. Watras to agree to the plan, formed committees, designed some flyers and ad-sale forms, and even sold one ad — the second trombonist said his parents would buy half a page for their jewelry store. Truly astounding. It was like seeing Bill Gates at age thirteen, times two. And half of him was wearing a cheerleader uniform.

Yes, I know that's a weird image.

On the way home, I thanked Annette for the idea. She was flying high; I think because now she really was a big part of the concert again. I wasn't sure how I felt. On the one hand, I knew the money would be a big plus for my family, and it would be great for Jeffrey to have a big special night. On the other hand, I was concerned that my parents might go nuts and trash the whole idea. Plus, and I know this is shallow, I wanted the concert to be MY big night.

One thing was for sure: One way or another, if my 'rents didn't veto the entire shebang, it was going to be important.

As I got out of the van, the driver said, *Listen, kid, I couldn't help overhearing about your brother. That's a tough break. I'm really sorry.*

Now, here was a lady who had driven the two of us to and from rehearsal twice a week for over a year, and this was the first time she had ever talked at all. It was a relief to know she had the power of speech, but I was struck again by the power of cancer to get attention. For better or for worse, being involved with cancer puts you on everybody's radar screen.

Now I had the challenge of floating this proposal to the 'rents, and I had to do it right away, because my mom and Jeffrey were leaving for Philly in the morning. At dinner, even while I was joking around with Jeffrey, fielding questions from my mom about schoolwork and wondering how my dad could have such a blank facial expression without actually being in a coma, I was nervously waiting for the opportunity to bring the whole thing up. Finally, I seized the day (or "carpe'ed" the "diem," if you wanted some Miss Palma lingo). My dad mentioned that he had gotten somebody a $7,000 tax return, and I pounced.

Wow, Dad, $7,000 sounds like a lot of money, huh?

Why, yes, Steven, it is.

I know a family that could get nearly three times that by April 15th.

Who?

Us!

Well, son, our return won't be THAT big this year. We are going to get some money back because your mother stopped working, and I hadn't claimed the single-earner head-of-household exemption. Also, the interest on our stock dividends will be less than we had projected. It's rather interesting; I had based our estimated taxes on a historical rate of return of approximately 10% annual yield. However, when the stock market slowed down, we actually had a negative rate of . . .

Dad, Dad, Dad, stop with the accounting talk for a minute. You're talking to a thirteen-year-old who got a thirty-seven on his math final, remember? Anyway, that's not what I meant. I'm talking about an idea that some people had. See, the All-City band needed a human service project, and a couple of the students came up with an amazing plan for one. Since we have this performance coming up, they thought, "Why not make it a benefit concert?"

A benefit concert? For whom?

Well . . . ummm . . . for US.

Jeffrey, please go into the family room and play.

Uh-oh.

But, Daddy, I'm still eating my burrito.

You get plenty of food. Go!

Double uh-oh.

Well, I had found a topic that put an expression on my father's face. It might have been nice if the expression weren't the teeth-gritted grimace of a sumo wrestler about to charge, but, hey — progress is progress, I suppose.

We argued back and forth about this for a while. Initially, my mom was on my dad's side, but as the "discussion" (It's amazing — my parents call everything a discussion. If I were standing across the street, firing a bazooka at my mother, while my father was launching mortars back at me, and Jeffrey was charging down the driveway with a grenade in his teeth, my parents would say we should stop having this public "discussion.") wore on, my mom got quieter and quieter. Eventually, before my father and I degenerated to the "Oh, yeah? YEAH!" level, she stopped us.

I think I'm going to be ill.

What do you mean, ill? Honey, Steven and I didn't mean to upset you; we were just having a discussion. (Sure. And Mount Everest is a "hill.")

No, I mean ill. As in, get me a bucket.

Triple uh-oh.

Steven, don't just sit there. Get her a . . . a . . . what can he get you?

Uuuuggghhhh! Men!

With that, she stumbled out of the dining room. When she turned on the super-loud bathroom fan, we knew exactly what was going on. And that left a fairly urgent problem. Jeffrey figured it out fastest. He appeared in the doorway.

Daddy, Steven, if Mommy is sick, who's going to take me to the hospital tomorrow?

Quadruple uh-oh. Who *was* going to take him?

A MEN'S JOURNEY

*A*s it turned out, my dad and I were both going to Philadelphia with Jeffrey. My mom couldn't take care of me at home and be violently sick at the same time, and my grandparents were away, so the 'rents couldn't dump me with them again. Of course, Jeffrey was thrilled.

Wow, Steven, we're going on a MEN'S JOURNEY tomorrow. Me, you, Daddy — this is going to be great. Wait till my methotrexate drip starts: We'll get to watch Shrek *and* Peter Pan *right IN A ROW if we want! And then we'll say my stomach hurts, and we'll both get Jell-O. And you can ride a REAL wheelchair! And then you can come to play-therapy with me! And if you want, you can go to the cafeteria during my vincristine push if the throwing up will bother you. I'll try to be brave, though. I promise. Do you think we could play cards while we wait for my EMLA to work? I love Go Fish. That's what Mommy usually plays with me. Do you know how to play it?*

Meanwhile, my mom was upstairs, taking a break from hurling so she could brief my dad.

OK, honey, make sure they give you the EMLA cream as soon as you get there. Remember, it takes an hour to numb his skin completely, so you have to get it on there right away. Jeffrey likes if you spread it over his port yourself but don't forget to warm it up between your hands first so it won't be cold on his skin. Then they'll flush the port and do the blood work. Jeffrey doesn't mind seeing the blood drawn, but you might want to send Steven on an errand so he won't have to look at it. He hated watching them access Jeffrey's port at the emergency room that time. Oh, what's next? The oncologist will probably come in to ask you some questions before we start the methotrexate. I'll write a note tonight, but you can basically tell him that Jeffrey hasn't been vomiting as much, and his CNS seems fine. He'll know what that means. Ooohhh, I forgot: If it's Dr. Arena, hold Jeffrey's hand. Jeffrey is afraid of him. If it's Dr. Moses, you're OK. He's Jeffrey's favorite. Speaking of favorites, Jeffrey loves the snow cones from the third-floor lounge. He swears they taste better than the ones on his floor. . . .

After a head-swimming twenty minutes of this,

my mom had to run back into the bathroom, but even then you could faintly hear her.

. . . and tell Dr. Moses to call Dr. Purow as soon as the CBCs come down. Dr. Purow has a question about the Leucovorin dosage.

Then she had to stop giving orders for a while as sickness overcame her. It was going to be a long few days for all of us.

Hours later, as I was lying in bed, I realized that my dad still hadn't given a final ruling on the benefit concert. Then I started thinking about the bills and about what I would see the next day at the hospital and about the schoolwork I would miss by being absent. Needless to say, it took hours to fall asleep. When I finally did, I had the Dream. As always, I woke up screaming, but this was even worse than usual. Because my mom was sick, she didn't come rushing in. By the time my dad got there, I had woken up by myself, sat bolt upright, smashed my head into my nightstand somehow, and bitten through the inside of my left cheek. I looked at my alarm clock, which was now blinking upside-down on the floor,

229 . . . 229 . . . 229. As my father patted me awkwardly on my sweat-drenched back and my breathing slowed down to near-normal, I thought, "Well, I might be gushing blood, but at least, I can get a few more hours of sleep." Then my dad leaned over, flipped the clock, and put it back on the table. That was when I realized it was really 6:22. Not only was it too late to get more sleep — it was too late, period. The day had started, with a bang AND a whimper.

Before I knew it, my father, Jeffrey, and I were all bundled into the car, along with my school books for studying, my sticks and practice pad, and extra clothes for all of us. Naturally, in the rush, we had forgotten something major, but we didn't know it yet. Dad was just trying to handle the pages and pages of notes my mom had heroically composed in the midst of her own bout of illness, Jeffrey was working on balancing a cup of juice and a Go-GURT while eating breakfast in his booster seat, and I was sucking on an ice cube in a sad attempt to stop the bleeding from my gouged cheek. I hope that none of the neighbors were watching this scene: the obviously sick lady swaying on the lawn in an old bathrobe, waving good-bye to the unshaven guy with the mis-buttoned dress shirt, who was driving two bald kids while one of them was intermittently spitting blood out the passenger-side window. Other than our chaos, it was so quiet on the block, you could almost hear the tick, tick, tick of the property values dropping as passersby took in the tableau of horror.

When we were about a mile from home, my dad noticed that the fuel light on the dashboard was blinking, so we stopped to get gas. I pumped while my father ran into the station to get a cup of coffee, so he could spill it on himself pulling out of the lot.

Then, just as we started down the on ramp for the highway, Jeffrey shouted, *I forgot Matt Medic! I forgot Matt Medic!*

Sorry, Jeff, I don't have time to turn us around. As it is, we're barely going to have time to spread that ookla cream on your port in time.

It's EMLA, Dad. But I NEED Matt Medic. He helps keep the bad blasts from coming back. I need him!

Not today, Jeffrey.

But, Dad . . .

The car lurched and veered into a driving lane in what might optimistically be referred to as a "close merge," and my dad replied through those famous clenched teeth, *Don't "but Dad" me right now, OK? I'm trying to drive in traffic, we're late, I got about three hours of sleep, I haven't shaved, I have no idea what I'm doing, and I'm SITTING IN A PUDDLE OF BOILING-HOT COFFEE!*

A year ago, Jeffrey would have been good for about another half-hour of whining, but now he just sat back with a sigh and sipped his juice. After a while, he assigned me a job for the duration.

Steven, it looks like Matt Medic is out of action. You have a new mission!

I slurred back, while desperately trying to avoid having my teeth touch the gaping hole in my cheek. *What is it, Buddy?*

Keep me brave. Please? Just keep me brave.

Then he finished his little meal and fell asleep, just like that. I stared out the window and wondered why Jeffrey thought I, of all people, was somehow qualified to keep *him* brave. You'd think his first choice might be somebody who didn't wake up crying in a pool of sweat every other day, or perhaps somebody who could sleep through the night in a soft bed without injuring himself. On the other hand, I supposed his first choice was actually an inanimate injection-molded plastic figurine. And as a second choice, I guessed I would have to do.

As we approached the hospital, we drove through the campus of the University of Pennsylvania. It was beautiful. Spring was just getting in gear, and there were happy college students walking everywhere in jeans and T-shirts, sweaters with shorts, miniskirts. Despite the early hour, I even saw a group of guys playing Frisbee. And I thought how weird it was for Jeffrey to be driving past all these carefree people who had it made, on his way to fight the twenty-seventh installment of a life-and-death battle against cancer. Good thing I was around to cheer my brother up with my positive outlook, huh?

We parked, and Jeffrey guided my father through

the check-in procedure. Then he led us upstairs to his floor. I paused for a minute in front of a set of double doors — I had imagined and feared the sights beyond them for months on end, but now it was time to face them. We pushed through, and stepped into Baldville, USA. There were sick kids everywhere — walking with IV poles, playing games, lying in beds, watching TV, sleeping. I had known I'd see lots of hairless little Jeffreys there, but there were kids of *all* ages. Some were older than me, some were probably in grade school, and a few were infants, which made me catch my breath. Some seemed healthier than Jeffrey, and others were in such bad shape that they had to be pushed around in wheelchairs. There were a lot of family members, too, but my eyes kept being drawn back to the patients. I was especially shaken by the sight of a girl who was probably my age. She was leaning against the wall in a robe, talking on a cell phone, even though you weren't supposed to use cell phones in the hospital. Her hair was almost gone, and her body was just a wisp, but you could tell that she had been gorgeous before the cancer. I hoped she'd be gorgeous again. She looked over at me with these pale blue eyes that you could tell had a lot going on behind them. I looked away and hurried to catch up to Jeffrey.

While my father and Jeffrey were getting set up in the room, I kind of hovered near the door. A friendly-looking, youngish lady came up to me. Her name tag said, ANDREA MCDERMOTT, CHILD LIFE SPECIALIST. She started right into a conversation.

A little overwhelming, isn't it? I'm Andi. You must be Jeffrey's brother, Steven. He talks about you all the time. He's a brave little guy.

You know him?

Yes, I check in on him every week. Sometimes, I get him into an art class or a story time or a game hour. Other times, we just talk or play cards.

Go Fish, right?

Yup. I guess he enlists you to play, too. Listen, you probably have about half an hour before Jeffrey is ready for treatment. Would you like to visit the chapel?

Ummm . . . why?

Well, your mother spends a lot of time there whenever Jeffrey is asleep or occupied, so I thought you might want to also.

Mom prays for Jeffrey? Of course, Mom would pray for Jeffrey. But somehow it hadn't occurred to me that she had a whole routine for it.

No, thanks. I think I'll stick around in case my brother needs me.

OK. I'm glad to finally meet you. Jeffrey thinks the world of you, and I can see why.

The morning was like that: hang around, stare at people, distract Jeffrey for a while, meet random new people who know all about my brother, stare some more. The amazing thing was how comfortable Jeffrey was there. I mean, it seemed like a very nice place, and I was glad so many people cared about him, but I couldn't imagine feeling *that* at home in a cancer ward.

We ate lunch while Jeffrey was getting his methotrexate, whatever that was. Evidently, this medicine was going to drip into him for twenty-four hours, and then they would give him other drugs to minimize the poisoning he would get from *this* drug. Anyway, after lunch my dad went to talk with the doctors. Jeffrey and I were watching *Shrek* on video when all of a sudden an alarm started clanging away. I must have jumped about a foot, but Jeffrey barely blinked.

Jeffrey, what's that? Is there a fire? Should I get you out of here?

He didn't even look away from the TV. *It's just a code, Steven. It happens all the time.*

A "code"? Wasn't that like on those TV hospital shows, when somebody . . .

Just then, a whole squadron of medical people ran by the open room door, carrying all sorts of equipment and shouting directions at each other. I was sure then: A "code" was when a patient's heart stopped. All of those doctors and nurses were charging down the hall to try and jump-start a child's heart. And Jeffrey saw this so often that it didn't even tear him away from his movie.

The day went on with an unlikely combination of boredom, anxiety, and bland food that you only find in hospitals. By early evening, as Jeffrey was dozing off and my father was talking with yet another medical person about something, I couldn't stand to be sitting in the room anymore. I grabbed my sticks and pad and set out in search of a private place to practice. In a hidden little alcove at the very end of the hall, I found a tiny room with washers and dryers. I guess it was there so families could do their laundry during long stays, but I had my own mission going on. I sat on top of the washer, put the pad on top of the dryer, hooked the door shut with an outstretched foot, and started running through my rudiments. It felt great to be concentrating on myself again, and the mindless repetition was relaxing; I must have played for about forty-five minutes nonstop. Then somebody banged on the door, which startled the heck out of me. I half-jumped, half-fell off of the washing machine. As I reached for the door, I dropped my sticks with a massive clatter. At the same moment, I realized I had once again bitten my cheek in the exact same place and that it was bleeding like a stuck pig. I swung the door open with a semi-angry

"WHHAAATTT?" Guess who was standing there, looking somewhat taken aback by the blood-drooling, shaved-headed madman in the closet? The girl I had seen that morning. She was wearing jeans and an Aéropostale sweatshirt instead of the robe, but those eyes were unmistakable.

Ummm . . . hey. I didn't mean to bother you. I just wanted to see what was going on; there's not much action around here at night.

Yeah, I'd noticed. I'm sorry I yelled. I just kind of zone out when I'm playing.

I listened for a while before I knocked. You're very fast. Hi, I'm Samantha.

Hi. I'm Steven. My brother Jeffrey is . . .

Yeah, everybody here knows Jeffrey. He's quite a character. Did he tell you about the time he kissed the night nurse?

Oops.

Anyway, he talks about you all the time: Steven the Rock Star. So when I heard the drumming, I kinda figured it might be you. By the way, did you know you're bleeding?

Uhhh, yeah. Do you want to come with me to get some ice?

Sure. There's a snow-cone machine on the other end of the hall, but it's not as good as . . .

The one on the third floor. I've heard.

So we got our snow cones and sat in the little kids' play lounge to talk. At some point, my dad saw me there but kept walking into Jeffrey's room. Nobody interrupted our conversation, and we talked until after midnight. I told her everything about my year — Renee, Annette, drums, school, Jeffrey, Jeffrey, and Jeffrey. And she told me everything, too: Just like Jeffrey, she had ALL. But unlike Jeffrey, she had had two relapses of her leukemia in the past four years. Now she was tired all the time, she rarely got to leave the hospital, and her bones were starting to ache every minute of every day. Things didn't look good.

How is your family doing with all this?

Well, my mom is a single parent, and we almost never hear from my dad. I have one older sister — she's away at college. We used to be really, really close. I still call her on my cell phone every few days, but she never stays on long. She hasn't visited me here since Christmas, but she promised she'd fly home in May to see me for my birthday. I hope she does. It kind of sounds stupid, but when I was little, I tried to do everything just like her. She used to love ice-cream cakes, so I loved them, too. For a couple of years after I got sick, she used to bring me an ice-cream cake on my birthday. Last year, she couldn't make it home. I mean, she had a good reason and every-thing — it was finals time at college — but it sucks having hospital cake for your birthday. It really sucks.

I'm sorry.

You don't have to be sorry — you didn't do anything wrong. You're HERE for your brother.

Well, I guess I am, but I get mad at him sometimes, and I haven't been here with him before today.

Well, you're here for him now. Believe me, that counts for something.

We talked for a while more after that, about all kinds of stuff: music, the opposite sexes, school (although she had been absent for months and had switched over to a tutor at the hospital), family. It's funny — I always think my life is so massively boring, but she wanted to know every little detail. It was like she was so hungry for a normal eighth grader's experiences that she needed to drink in mine. Every once in a while, especially as it got later and her last dose of painkillers wore off, she would flinch for a second, but her eyes never lost the intensity I had noticed earlier. At some point, we both got really sleepy, but nobody wanted to break the spell that encircled our little couch amid the rainbow-colored animals and crayon boxes. Finally, a nurse came in to give Samantha a cup full of pills, and things changed. When the nurse walked back out, the mood had vanished, and we were just two bald kids on a sofa.

We started that whole "I ... uhhh ... ooohhh, look at the time" thing that grown-ups always do when they're breaking away from an awkward encounter at the supermarket. Before we went our separate ways, though, Samantha had one more thing to tell me.

Stay with your brother, Steven. Stay with him. No matter what. Do you promise?

What was I going to do? I promised.

As Samantha turned to start her slow walk back to her room, I had a last idea. I ran after her, told her to wait right there, charged down the hallway to the laundry room, got my drum stuff, and galloped back.

Here, Sam. I want you to have these sticks. They're my favorite pair for practicing: Pro-Mark 5A hickory with nylon tips. Keep 'em, and maybe I can give you lessons when I come down. Would that be cool?

Steven, thank you. That would be great.

Happy early birthday, Samantha.

Happy early birthday, Samantha.

I'M A MAN NOW

The next day was really busy, with Jeffrey's treatment and a million and one doctors coming into the room. So I didn't see Samantha at all through the whole morning and afternoon. I was planning to stop by her room and say good-bye, but I got distracted on the way out. I overheard the main guy, Dr. Moses, giving my dad a pretty strong warning as we were getting ready to leave.

Listen, Mr. Alper, I've been on and off the phone with your son's pediatrician all morning. I'm concerned about Jeffrey's hepatic function. His ALT has climbed sharply over the past week, and I want Dr. Purow to keep an eye on your son's blood counts and transaminase numbers for the next couple of weeks — if the AST climbs, too, we'll need to know about it. Of course, we'll be running our own tests every week here, but liver trouble is nothing to mess around with, and I want to be extremely cautious as long as Jeffrey is on such high doses of 6-MP and methotrexate.

I'm sorry, Doctor, but my wife is the one who has been handling all of the medical stuff so far. Can you explain that?

OK, "hepatic" equals "liver." The liver's job is to filter the blood. When a child is on as many heavy-duty chemotherapy drugs as Jeffrey is, the liver takes a beating. We check the blood levels of certain enzymes periodically in order to make sure that the liver is handling the strain adequately. If the liver begins to sustain damage, the enzyme levels should theoretically give us some warning. Then we have to adjust the patient's meds until we get the chemo regimen in balance with the patient's liver function. Otherwise, there is a risk of liver failure, which can be fatal.

That was just peachy. "THEORETICALLY give us some warning." Sheesh!

So Jeffrey's liver tests aren't . . . uhhh . . . so good right now?

They're really not great.

So what do we have to do?

You'll need to bring your son to a lab for blood work three days from now; Dr. Purow has all the details.

That's routine in a case like this. Just to be on the safe side, keep this in mind for the future: If you think Jeffrey is looking at all yellow, in his skin tone or around the eyes, bring him in immediately. Also, as always, if he suddenly spikes a fever over the next few weeks, he will be in need of urgent care.

Urgent care?

Yes. You will need to drop everything and get him to the E.R. — no matter where you are, no matter what you are doing. Got it?

Yes, Doctor.

One more thing, Mr. Alper: Don't worry. You have a coordinated team of doctors monitoring this situation very closely.

You have to love it when the doctor lays all this horrific stuff on you and then tells you not to worry. It's like saying, "Here's thirty-seven pounds of assorted chocolates. Try not to think about food, though." Or "Look! There's Renee Albert in a bikini. But please try to keep your mind on algebraic functions."

So you can see why I didn't have time to drop in on my new friend, Sam. As we were walking out of the ward with all our stuff, I heard some clicking sounds; she was trying out her new drumsticks. I was hoping that I really could give her a lesson next time I came down with Jeffrey. And, thanks to her, I was sure there would *be* a next time.

In the car on the way home, my dad didn't say much until we got clear of the heavy Philadelphia traffic and Jeffrey fell asleep.

Then he turned to me and said, *Look, ummm, I want to thank you for coming down to support Jeffrey. Maybe I haven't been saying it, but I'm really very proud of you. You're turning into a good man.*

Wow! "A good man." You caught that, correct? Steven is a *man* now. Quick, somebody tell all the chicks and babes at school for me!

And I've been thinking about this concert thing. I know how much your music means to you, and I also know that you will be doing this for the right reasons. So even though I really don't think we need the help, you can go ahead with it. I'm not sure I'll be able to go, with all the tax work I have to do this month and all, but I'm behind you in your decision.

YOU AREN'T GOING to my concert?

I'm just not sure, Steven. I have a lot to get caught up on, and you know that these last few weeks before April 15th are crunch time for accountants every year. I'll, uhhh, I'll do my best.

My first thought when he said that was, "Wonderful. Now that I'm a *man,* my dad can weasel his way out of going to my concerts. What next? Maybe he'll stop buying food for me, or rent out my room."

Then, for possibly the first time since all of this had started, I stopped feeling sorry for myself and thought of other people's situations. It could have been worse: I could have been Annette, who had practiced all year for a concert she wouldn't play in, or Sam, who might be dying all by herself in the hospital while her sister parties it up at college. Or Jeffrey.

Speaking of Jeffrey, you should have seen how my mother charged straight to him when we pulled into the driveway. I guess she had gotten her strength back while we were gone, because she lifted Jeffrey up in a rib-crushing hug until he practically begged her to let him down. I guess I was still in my new, manly sympathetic mood, because normally I would have been standing around saying, "Ahem," until my mom noticed me, too, but that day I just looked at her with a new appreciation. This woman had spent nearly half of her time this year at the hospital with her son, praying for him, watching over him, comforting him, handling all of this overwhelming cancer stuff. And suddenly, as she reached out and squeezed my arm, I realized without any shadow of a doubt that she would have done the same for me.

Maybe you'll think it's nuts that the brother of a cancer patient would feel lucky, but at that instant, I most surely did.

The next three weeks of school were absolutely nutty. Annette and Renee both insisted on tutoring me in the subjects I had missed during my two days in Philadelphia. I let Renee in the house this time. They also insisted on updating me daily on the progress of the benefit concert, to the point where the details were just too much: "The posters are up all over town. We called the newspaper; they said they'll send a reporter to the last rehearsal and the concert. The high school band has already sold 286 tickets. Your brother's school took out a full-page ad in the program. Dexter's Auto Body bought a double-page spread . . ." I was half-expecting them to tell me how many lightbulbs the high school stage had, what colors the bulbs were, how much heat they gave off in kilojoules, and whether that was greater than or less than the total caloric output of the school cafeteria on any given day, with and without the snack line. But I knew they meant well and that in a sense they were doing all of this for me.

My teachers and fellow students were all over me, too. "I bought a ticket to your concert." "I bought two tickets to your concert." "I bought seven tickets and rented six strangers and a minivan for the night." Again, everybody meant well, and I was really hoping that the money this raised would take a load off of my parents' shoulders, but the intensity of all the attention was pretty high. I just couldn't wait to actually get up there and play the drums for all these people — that was the part *I* was living for, anyway.

And if excessive amounts of rehearsal time were any indication of success, we were surely destined to go down in jazz history. There were practices four days a week for the last few weeks. In fact, if I had spent any more time with the van driver (who was bringing just about everyone she knew to the concert), I swear I would have started calling her Mom. Plus, I was still taking lessons on Saturdays from Mr. Stoll (who was bringing seven students to the concert), AND practicing on my own, both at home and during my opportunity periods at school. AND I was doing all of my homework. My math teacher (who was planning to bring a small army of anal-retentive, calculator-carrying, math-teacher children to the concert) even commended me for my improved work habits.

Speaking of improved work habits, I was also spending a ton of time reading. Mrs. Galley (four tickets, one booster ad) had called me down right before my big trip to the hospital with Jeffrey. She'd said she just wanted to check in with me, but then she'd immediately pushed the candy dish my way, so I knew there was a heavy topic on the agenda. It turned out that she had ordered a book for me to read, about childhood leukemia and its treatment. She said she thought it might help me to "process my feelings." I thanked her, snatched up some candy hearts, and walked out with the book under my arm. At the time, my thought was, "Yeah, like I'm really in the mood to read a book about this when I'm living it 24/7 already."

But after we got back from the hospital, I had picked up the book again, because I truly did want to understand what was going on with my brother and with Samantha, too. It was about six hundred pages long, but I was already halfway through. And somebody else had been reading it every night after I went to bed: my dad. I think reading it was helping both of us. It was like Mrs. Galley had said, "I want to leave you with one thing to think about: Instead of agonizing about the things you can't change, why don't you try working on the things you *can* change?" We couldn't change the fact that Jeffrey was sick, but we could make sure we knew what was going on. And if there was one thing I'd finally figured out, it was that your mind is something you always CAN change.

And so, everyone was rallying around Jeffrey. Everything was going well. Jeffrey's next three hospital stays were uneventful, and his blood counts and liver-function tests were steady — not great, but steady. Life was going about as well as could possibly be expected, right up until the day of the concert.

ROCK STAR

As fate would have it, the last time I ever had the Dream was early in the morning on Friday, April 4th. That was the day of the concert, so it might have been nice to have slept well — but by the time I had showered the Dream away and headed downstairs for breakfast, I was so nervously hyper that there was no way a lack of sleep was going to slow me down. I would just have to crash on Saturday.

My mom and Jeffrey were down in Philadelphia, but they were due to get back in time for the concert. My dad and I had never spoken again about his choice not to attend the concert, but I know my mom and he had had at least one "discussion" about it — the kind of discussion that rattles your teeth, that you can't help overhearing no matter how loud you crank your Discman. So that morning, when the issue was on both of our minds, he and I didn't have a single safe word to say to each other. It was weird being so nervous and so quiet at the same time, but as soon as I got to school, the "quiet" part became a memory. Renee assaulted me in homeroom with a copy of the program in her hand. It was thicker than any school program I had ever seen, with a beautiful, glossy cover shot of the band onstage. When you opened the program, there was Jeffrey. His kindergarten photo was blown up nearly to full-page size, and beneath it, there was a statement in neat black calligraphy: "All proceeds from tonight's concert will benefit the Jeffrey Alper Medical Trust." Simply unbelievable. Thanks to the amazing brains of two girls, Jeffrey had gone from being a regular little kid to being a "Medical Trust." I had to admit, despite the strangeness of the whole thing, Renee and Annette had done an incredible job with the whole project.

When the homeroom bell rang, Annette came rushing in to give me the latest totals on box office receipts and the profits from the program ads. As soon as she and Renee were standing together, I noticed that they had both gotten really short haircuts. REALLY short haircuts. But you know me by now — I just chalked it up to coincidence, thanked them for all their hard work, answered a few questions about Jeffrey, and went to class. That day, Miss Palma (three tickets and a gigantic basket of cookies for the bake sale) was showing a movie based on the last book we had read, so, of course, I spaced out completely. I couldn't even tell you what I thought about, but I'm pretty sure it wasn't Homer's use of foreshadowing in the *Odyssey*. Mostly, I think, I practiced playing the All-City songs in my head. Somehow, between Miss Palma saying, "Please take note of the dramatic irony in this scene," and my brain saying, "Bip bop dit dit doo-wah," I got through the class. The whole day was like that, but eventually even a Friday at middle school has to come to an end. The last bell rang, and I started to head out for the bus. Then the intercom in Mr. Watras's room buzzed, and I got called to the office.

Now THAT will put a lump in your throat, right? On the way there, I alternated between running (so I could find out the news fast) and trudging (so I wouldn't have to know yet). Either way, my mind never slowed down for a second: "Oh, geez. Grandma fell and broke her hip. Oh, God. Dad is here to kidnap me so I can't be at the concert. He'll probably set me up with a slide rule and a pile of tax returns in some cheesy motel by the interstate. All he has to do is hold me for about six hours, and it will all be over. My hopes, my dreams, my big conga solo — ruined! Plus, I hate math."

And while these surface thoughts were providing some distraction, I knew that the other nine-tenths of this mental iceberg, the deadly part that was hidden below, was all about Jeffrey.

When I got there, my mom and brother were standing by the chairs that bad kids sit in while they're waiting to get reamed out by the principal. My mom was chatting calmly with one of the secretaries, while the other was giving Jeffrey chocolates from a big jar on her desk. Naturally, I had been going to that school for three years without ever being offered candy from that lady's desk — but whatever. Jeffrey spotted me right away.

Steven, guess what? Today is your concert!

Yeah, buddy, I know. What's going on? Are you all right? Was your blood work OK?

I don't know. I'm only five. There was a clown in my hospital room today. He was pretty cool. He painted my face so I could be Spider-man. I wanted Green Power Ranger, but the clown said he didn't have enough green face paint. Isn't that weird? He wasn't such a prepared clown, I don't think.

I needed some facts, and I needed them pronto. Mom.

Don't interrupt, Steven.

Mom! Is everything OK?

Sure.

Then why are you here? Why did you page me and give me a heart attack?

We were on our way home, and I thought you might like to spend some time with your family on your big day. So we picked you up. Don't be so dramatic.

I'm not being dramatic, Mom. I was worried.

Well, worry no more. Your mother is on the scene, and everything is under control.

Yeah, things had been completely out of hand before she stepped in to rescue me heroically from my long, painful bus ride WITH ANNETTE AND RENEE.

Thanks for the thought, Mom. But you know, I AM entitled to a complimentary bus ride home at taxpayer expense. And I'd hate to disappoint the taxpayers, so I'll just be on my way, then.

Steven, wait! I want to see you. I missed you. They did me a spinal tap. It was scary!

Sigh. So long, my girls. Hello, my boy.

On the way home, my mother briefed me about Jeffrey's treatment. His counts still didn't look good, and Dr. Moses had almost kept him in the hospital for another few days. But when my mom told the doctor about the big concert, he had agreed to discharge Jeffrey with another specific warning to rush to the E.R. if anything didn't seem right. I was grateful to my mom for going to bat about this; with my dad refusing to attend, my fifteen minutes of fame would have been pretty lonely without her and Jeffrey. I mean, I would still have known, like, half the audience, and my grandparents weren't going to miss this for anything. But still, it was nice to know that I'd have a couple of relatives there who didn't need to chug a can of Geritol to stay awake for the whole performance.

For his part, Jeffrey did seem kind of wiped out. On the other hand, he was also definitely all psyched up to see me play. My mom had explained to him that the concert was going to raise money for his treatment, that he should thank people for coming, that he should behave himself like a gentleman, blah blah blah. But he hadn't been particularly interested in any of that; his big goal for the evening was to shout out, "Yay, Steven! THAT'S MY BROTHER!" every time I hit a drum.

Back at the house, we still had about an hour and a half to kill before I was supposed to be at the high school. I was a madman. I paced back and forth in my room, laying out, refolding, and double-checking my clothes (All-City Jazz Band T-shirt and black jeans), as if there were a way to screw up the putting on of a uniform. Then I stalked downstairs to the kitchen and laid out three different snack cakes, agonizing over which one would provide the best musical energy boost. "Well, the chocolate-covered, chocolate-filled chocolate doughnut provides both sugar and caffeine. Yet the vanilla snack cake is even sweeter, for that quick burst of power. And what of the classic apple pie? It is individually wrapped in waxed paper for freshness and probably provides traces of at least one vitamin." In the end, my mother walked in and insisted I eat a yogurt, as if THAT were food. I knew the band would be having the traditional post-concert pizza delivered to the rehearsal room, but honestly — was I supposed to survive on nothing but bacteria-laden milk solids for the next several hours?

A compromise was reached, and I am pleased to report that vanilla yogurt makes quite an edible topping for apple pie.

I bounced around the house, trying not to wake Jeffrey, who had dozed off on the living-room couch. I read *Modern Drummer Magazine* for five-minute stretches. In between, I paced some more.

Occasionally, I peeked out the front window in the hope that my father had changed his mind and was at that very moment pulling up to the house. But who was I kidding?

The time crawled by like a tortoise with arthritis, but finally the kitchen clock said 5:17. It was time to roll out. I shouted for my mom, woke Jeffrey up, ran upstairs, changed into my concert clothes, put on my shoes, and was standing by the door to the garage by 5:19 — chanting, "Let's go! Come *on!*" (Feel free to try that at home, by the way; moms love it!) I practically hurled Jeffrey into his booster seat and dove headlong into the car after him. I was in the mood to peel out, burn rubber, lay the pedal to the metal — I wanted my mom to SKID her way to the concert. Like, maybe we could get pulled over for speeding and my mom could tell the officer, "But, sir, do you know who's in the backseat? That's Steven Alper, *the* second drummer for All-City Jazz Band . . . and his concert starts in less than an hour!" Then the cop could dash back to his car, call headquarters, and get us a motorcycle escort to the high school.

Or my mom could just putt there at her usual, stately 31 miles per hour while Jeffrey and I bounced and chattered in the backseat like two bald monkeys on a sugar high.

Either way, I suppose, we wound up at the school. Jeffrey insisted on coming with me into the band room, which was his right, since the concert *was* for him. When we entered, I almost had a heart attack: Every single member of the band was wearing a matching red baseball cap. Did I miss a memo or something? HAD I screwed up my uniform after all? My mom looked at me. I looked at my mom. Jeffrey ran around the room, oblivious. And then somebody spoke. It was Biff, of all people.

Jeffrey, I have something to tell you. We, the members of the All-City jazz ensemble, would like to present you with a gift in honor of your courage, your good cheer, and the inspiration you give to all of us.

Well, that was laying it on with a trowel, but OK — he had our interest, anyway.

So, Jeffrey, we hereby proclaim you to be an honorary member of the band. It is my pleasure to give you this official All-City T-shirt AND this very special All-City ball cap.

He took off his own cap to give to Jeffrey. Underneath it, he was bald. Biff had shaved his head in tribute to my brother! Just as I started to get a mental grasp on this, everyone else reached for their hats, too. At a signal from Annette, who was standing with Renee by the piano, they all whipped off their hats as well. My mom was the only person in the room with hair long enough to comb. I flashed back to Annette and Renee's matching super-short dos, and suddenly, it all made sense. Suddenly, too, I had a huge lump in my throat. Jeffrey was running all over the room, hugging everyone, rubbing players' heads for good luck, and my mom was standing there next to Mr. Watras (whose natural baldness had excused him from the pre-show razoring festivities). There were unquestionably tears welling up in her eyes, but she also looked happy. Honestly, when I saw that look on my mom's face, I practically ran over to Biff and hugged him myself.

We hung out for a while. Jeffrey ran up to me and

buried his head in my stomach. I sort of wrestled free; he looked right up into my eyes and whispered, *You're the best drummer in the world.* Then my mom started walking out with him so they could find their reserved, front-and-center seats in the auditorium. When she pulled open the door, my dad almost fell into the room. He had made it after all! When he saw the roomful of bare scalps, though, he immediately got kind of a grim facial expression. He gave me a little half-wave, mumbled, "Good luck," and wheeled right back around to lead my mom and Jeffrey to their seats.

Hmmm ...

Mr. Watras gathered us all around, gave us a big pep talk, and led us downstairs onto the stage. The curtain was closed, so we had a few minutes to set up before everyone would see us. We all busied ourselves with the little things musicians do right before they play: testing spit valves, applying last-minute drops of valve oil, checking the lugs on the snare drum and the height of a cymbal. In short order, we were ready. I was nervous but glad that the big night was about to get started. I sat down behind the drum kit (I was playing set for the first tune), adjusted the sheet music on its stand, wiped my hands on a grubby little towel I always kept in my stick bag just for that purpose, and took a deep breath. Mr. Watras tapped his baton on the podium. The curtain opened.

When the shiny heads of the entire band became visible in the stage lights, the audience was dead silent. Then, as they began to realize what they were seeing, I could hear a buzz of whispers, then gasps, and then a slow-building crescendo of applause. Before we even played a note, we got a standing ovation. Mr. Watras let the applause rise, then fall a bit, and then — BAM! — he counted us right into the first tune: "Mambo Number Five" by Louis Prima. I don't really remember playing a single note of the first five or six songs; I can only recall the nonstop swell of emotion that we were all feeling — the band, Mr. Watras, the audience, and, I hoped, Jeffrey. Every song went better than the one before. Every solo got hotter and hotter, more and more beautiful.

The fast numbers were a riot of energy, and the ballads put the entire place into some kind of powerful, floating dream state. I've never experienced anything like it, but I knew that the entire point of playing music was to hope that once in a while you could bring *this* feeling to an audience of people.

When the curtain closed for intermission, the place went up again. It was great! We all took our time onstage, getting our instruments squared away, slapping fives, rubbing heads (weird sensation, by the way), and just basking in the success of the first set. Then Mr. W. told us to go back up to the band room to get drinks, hit the restrooms, and relax for a little while. I set up the congas at the height I liked; I was tired and thirsty, but I couldn't wait to come back down and play the Latin pieces I had been sweating over all year. Brian tapped me on the shoulder and gestured with his thumb toward the stairs. We walked up.

At the top of the steps, just outside of the band room, my mom was having what looked like an intense discussion with Mr. Stoll — maybe even a "discussion." She turned to me with the alarming fake-sweet smile she only uses when she's got me totally busted for something.

In the syrupy voice that always goes with the smile, she spoke to me. *You're playing very well tonight, Steven.*

Thanks, Mom.

Very well.

Ummm, thanks again.

Especially for a kid who hasn't paid for a drum lesson in over a month.

Ouch!

Then she surprised me, Mr. Stoll, and possibly even herself by grabbing me up in a bear hug.

You are a wonderful son, and a wonderful man.

Yet another parent busting forth with the "man" thing! I'd have to check my chest for signs of hair when I got home. Mr. Stoll broke the moment by pounding me on the shoulder.

You are rocking the joint, kiddo! I loved the big triplet

fill in "Satin Doll." And your four-limb independence is really coming along. I can't wait to hear the Dizzy Gillespie tune.

Then Mr. W. called all the band members into the room, so I thanked Mr. Stoll and hurried in. My dad and Jeffrey were there. Mr. Watras got everyone quiet, and then gestured to my dad. Evidently — and I couldn't believe this — my father wanted to address the band. He cleared his throat twice, paused for a long, uncomfortable moment, then spoke.

I almost didn't come here tonight. I'm a proud man, I guess, and I didn't like the idea of accepting charity.

I looked around and saw that the other kids and Mr. W. were looking rather nervous.

Even my wife couldn't get me to come. I was all ready to go to work, bury myself in a pile of paper, and tell myself I was helping my family by earning more money. But at about 5 o'clock, as everybody else in my office was leaving for the weekend to go home to their families, I realized that . . .

He faltered for a moment, and again I saw that people just didn't know how to take this speech.

I don't know . . . I guess I realized that my family needs a dad more than they need a few extra bucks. Jeffrey, my sweet little boy, needs me to be around to support him when he isn't feeling well. My wife over there needs me to be around to support her — all the time. And my big, talented boy over there, the one who's trying to stare at his shoes until I stop talking . . .

At this, there was some laughter.

He deserves to have his father see what an amazing musician he is. He's also an amazing brother and just an amazing guy. I know you all call him the Peasant . . .

More laughter.

. . . but I think he's a prince. Thank you, Steven, for watching out for your family, even when your father wasn't. And thank you, All-City members, for a great concert, a marvelous show of support, and . . . uhhh, listening to me ramble.

Once more, laughter. My mom walked over, holding Jeffrey's hand, and kissed my dad. It is always a little weird watching your 'rents kiss, even when it's not in a room full of people who actually KNOW you, but this was kind of nice. It occurred to me that that was the first time I'd seen them kiss in a while. Then I looked down at Jeffrey, who had a really miserable look on his face, like he was tasting something vile. Turns out, he was. The next moment, he ran over to the trash can and vomited into it. I ran over to him and got my arms around him. Just then, the lights blinked: Annette and Renee were at the door, bringing glad tidings of box office and bake sales. Without all of the receipts having been counted yet, the running total for the evening was already over $21,000. Half of the room cheered, while the other half — the half that had noticed Jeffrey's run — was just standing around, looking edgy once again. I wasn't really worried yet; Jeffrey's meds made him nauseous all the time. The real danger sign would be a fever. So I felt Jeffrey's forehead. It was really hot. I hated to say what I said next; I knew it was going to cause some trouble. But I also knew what the doctors had said about not delaying treatment at this point.

Uhhh, Mom. I think Jeffrey has a temp.

This set off a little wave of alarm. My parents knew somebody had to go rushing out of there with

Jeffrey to the E.R., but who? One of them? Both? And was I supposed to skip out on the biggest moment of my life and go with them? Jeffrey looked at me.

Steven, I feel really bad. And Matt Medic is at home again. Please come with me. I'm scared.

You know how sometimes, when you have a high-pressure decision to make, you feel like everybody is looking at you? Well, in this case, everybody really WAS looking at me. Annette. Renee. Mr. W. Mom. Dad. Jeffrey. Four trombone players, for God's sake! Was I supposed to walk out on the music for my brother? Or was I supposed to stay and play the concert?

I looked at all of the faces. I wasn't sure. I whipped my head in every direction, searching for some clue in the eyes around me. And then I got my clue, from a girl I had only ever met once. "Stay with your brother, Steven. Stay with him. No matter what. Do you promise?" I had promised Samantha I would be there for Jeffrey. There would be other concerts.

Mr. W., I have to . . .

I know. Go!

My eyes started to well up. *I'm sorry. I'm sorry. I was supposed to be your big star.*

Steven, you have never been MORE of a star to me than you are at this moment. Go. Take care of your brother. We'll be fine here.

Mom was on her way out the door; Dad was right behind her, carrying Jeffrey. I started after them, but Renee and Annette were right there in front of me. Renee hugged me and wished me luck. Then Annette put her casted hand on my shoulder. I wasn't sure what to say.

Some team we make, huh, Annette? You can't play the concert, and I could play but have to run out!

Then she put her good hand on my other shoulder and gave me something to wonder about.

She said, *I think we make a GREAT team!* And she kissed me on the cheek.

As I ran out of the room to chase after the distant backs of my parents, my mind was reeling. Annette had kissed me.

Who would'a thunk it?

THE END

An ear infection. Jeffrey had an ear infection. I missed the highlight of my year because Jeffrey had an ear infection.

Thank God. It could have been so much worse. We spent pretty much the whole night at the local emergency room, until Jeffrey's blood work came back at around 2 a.m. His white counts were low, but the doctor said that was probably just a response to the infection. His liver-function test results actually looked better than they had in weeks. So this was going to be just the usual, routine week-of-IV-antibiotics-in-Philly sickness; Jeffrey would be transported down there around two in the afternoon the next day. He had asked that I be allowed to ride down in the ambulance with him, and I was willing. They hadn't exactly said yes yet, but I had a feeling it was going to happen.

My dad and I went home to sleep for a few hours and pack my stuff. I collapsed into bed with my clothes on and didn't wake up until after 11 a.m. As soon as I went downstairs in the morning, I noticed that the answering machine was blinking. We had slept through a lot of phone calls! There were about a million messages from people who had been at the concert, wishing us well and checking on Jeffrey's health status. Here are a few that jumped out at me:

This is Judy Galley, Steven's counselor from the middle school, calling. I hope Jeffrey is feeling better. Steven, I was very proud of you tonight. When I first started working with you this year, you were so angry that I worried about you a lot, and you felt that you couldn't control your own life. Now you have accepted control of your own path and are doing a wonderful job of helping those around you, too. Just remember: Instead of agonizing about the things you can't change . . .

I hit fast forward — I absolutely knew the rest by heart.

Mr. Stoll here. I hope the little guy is OK. Steven, don't worry about leaving the concert. Max asked me to sit in and cover your parts, and I did. The band sounded great — it wasn't what it would have been with you there, but we all got by. OK, good night, dude. Will I see you at your lesson tomorrow?

Max? Oh, yeah — Mr. Watras.

This is Renee Albert. Hi, Steven. I hope your brother is OK. Hi, Mr. Alper. Hi, Mrs. Alper. Good news! We just finished totaling up the proceeds from the concert: TWENTY-THREE THOUSAND, FOUR HUNDRED EIGHTY-NINE DOLLARS AND SEVENTEEN CENTS!!! Steven, Mr. Watras is going to bring the check over later this week. I hope you let him in . . . just kidding!

This is Annette. I hope everything is all right there. Steven, call me when you can about . . . what happened, OK? You know, when you were leaving? I really . . . ummm . . . I really meant it. I just wanted you to know.

It was interesting, hearing Renee and Annette right in a row like that. Somehow, overnight, I had fig-ured something out: Renee was beautiful, but she was my friend now. On the other hand, Annette was my friend, but now she was beautiful.

Makes about as much sense as anything ever does when you're talking about girls, right?

The day started. I ate and showered. My father drove me to the hospital. I got to have my first ambulance ride — Jeffrey squeezed my hand with all his might for about forty miles. Good thing my drum lesson was canceled, because I wasn't sure I'd regain the feeling in my hand for a few days. Still, that was okay; I knew if I hadn't been there he'd have had nothing to squeeze.

We got to Philly. My mom met us. Jeffrey got installed in a room. His IV bags got hung. I stayed with him until he fell asleep for a nap. Then I tiptoed out and went down the hall to say hi to Samantha and tell her how I had followed through on my promise to her. But when I got to her room, it was empty, and the bed was stripped.

The next few minutes are a blur. I grabbed the little cord that calls the nurse and buzzed and buzzed nonstop until a lady came charging in.

She said in that semi-scary nurse voice, *What's wrong?*

My voice came out all quiet and wobbly. *Ummm, there was a patient here. Her name is Samantha. She's my friend. Now she's not here, but she said she's always in this room. Did she get sent home?*

The nurse looked uncomfortable. *Well . . .*

And then I knew.

She's dead? She died? ANSWER ME!

Yes, she . . . passed away early yesterday morning.

She wasn't alone, was she? Was her mother with her?

Yes, as far as I know, her mother was with her . . . at the end.

Was her sister with her?

The nurse looked puzzled. *Sister?*

That's when I lost it. I sat down, started crying and shouting and pounding on the floor, and refused to get up. Somewhere in there, the nurse called for a social worker. Somewhere in there, my mom came running. Somewhere in there, another nurse came in with a wrapped package about a foot and a half long, addressed from Samantha to me. My mom opened it in front of me. Samantha had returned my Pro-Mark 5A's with a note: "Thank you for the company, and for the loan. Please think of me when you use these, OK? Love, Sam."

Oh, God. Now I would always have two pairs of Special Sticks.

EPILOGUE

Annette is sitting to the left of me; Renee is on my right. It's two months later, and I'm on the outdoor stage at my eighth-grade graduation ceremony. We're in those special seats for kids who win the big awards. It's about nine hundred degrees out, and my giant poofy brown gown is sticking to my arms like plastic wrap. But even though the baking sun is slowly laminating me, I am happy. I've been thinking over this whole year in one gigantic rush, so I'm sure I've missed some key moments in the principal's speech. Suddenly, there's an awfully sharp elbow slamming into my ribs.

"Clap, Steven!"

Annette has that my-boyfriend-is-from-space look that I've been coming to know pretty well lately. I snap back to reality and realize that Renee is standing to get her certificate.

"This year's Outstanding Achievement in Mathematics Award goes to . . . Renee Albert!"

As Renee swishes back into her seat — and I must admit she can still swish in a world-champion kind of way — Annette jabs me again, right in the same spot. I'm up.

"The Outstanding Musical Achievement Award goes to . . . Steven Alper!"

I walk toward the podium for my big handshake moment as Annette and Renee applaud wildly. I don't swish like Renee, but at least I don't trip over my gown and go tumbling off the stage into the front row. As I sit back down, I have to laugh a little. I may be the only kid in America who ever clinched the Musical Achievement Award by skipping out on his big concert. I guess maybe my biggest achievement was learning that there's more to life than taking the big drum solo.

One more elbow jab, and I'm clapping again.

"I am especially honored to bestow our first-ever Human Service Award to . . . Annette Watson!"

Renee stands up; she's still clapping at top speed. Annette stops after her handshake and looks around. Just as Renee bends down to elbow me on the other side of my rib cage, I realize that I'm virtually the only person on the entire football field whose butt is still touching a chair. Annette has gotten a standing ovation. I jump up, too, and the standing O is unanimous. Annette starts walking back toward us, and call me crazy, but I think I'm detecting some swishing going on. When she gets back to her seat, she reaches out to hold my hand. We're both totally sweaty, but I kinda like it.

Before I know it, I'm getting a tremendous double-sided elbow attack. I jump up as I realize it's time for that hat-throwing thing you always see in the movies. For some reason, I look out into the audience to where my family is sitting, about thirty-three rows back. Jeffrey has jumped up, too, and is holding the brim of his baseball cap. At the instant I throw my cap up, he tosses his. There's this amazing moment when both are hovering maybe twenty feet in the air. I look at Jeffrey, and even though he's so far away, I know he's looking at me, too. From here, I can barely make out the inch or two of new blond hair on his head, but I know it's there.

Just as our caps start to tumble back down, a huge cloud of balloons goes up. We're all cheering. Annette is hugging me, Renee is pounding on my back, my 'rents are on their feet, too. The recessional music begins, and we all start the shuffling-out-up-the-aisle thing. When I finally reach row 33, I want to stop and bask in the view of my mom and dad, Jeffrey, and my grandparents all standing together for me.

But I also know that if I stopped, I'd get trampled by the two hundred pairs of feet that are trudging along behind me, so I only pause for a moment. Jeffrey runs over to the aisle to slap me five, and our eyes lock. He starts to speak — I can't hear the words over the shouts, the clapping, and the roar of the band, but I'm a good lip-reader.

"I love you, Steven."

Suddenly, I'm blinking furiously, like there's something caught in my eye. Before I have this mysterious vision issue under control, I'm about twenty rows past Jeffrey, so I've missed the moment for a quick reply.

That's OK. I know Jeffrey knows how I feel. I

know that, in the middle of everything else that's gone swirling around us this year, I've been his play buddy, dropped everything for him, held his hand whenever he's asked. As I walk out of the stadium to the grass where my classmates are milling about, wondering which way to start the next big walk into our futures, I think about Samantha. She died without a sister by her side — but she also made sure that Jeffrey would live with a brother by *his*. And, of course, she showed me a thing or two.

It's funny. I used to think that having a brother was the worst thing in the world. But now I know that not having him would be worse. He comes running out of the stadium behind me, ahead of my parents, and slams into my legs like a 3-foot-tall express train.

I turn to him and start to tell him the words I will now, thankfully, have time to say. "Jeffrey, I . . ."

About the Author

Jordan Sonnenblick attended amazing schools in New York City. Then he went to an incredible Ivy League university and studied very, very hard. However, due to his careful and well-planned course selection strategies, he emerged from college with a fancy-looking diploma and a breathtaking lack of real-world skills or employability.

Thank goodness for Teach for America, a program that takes new college graduates, puts them through "teacher boot camp," and places them at schools around the country with teacher shortages. Through TFA, Mr. Sonnenblick found his place in the grown-up world, teaching adolescents about the wonders and joys — the truth and beauty — of literature.

Mr. Sonnenblick always wanted to be a writer, too, so one day in 2003 he started the book that became *Drums, Girls & Dangerous Pie*. He was inspired to write the book by the story of one of his students whose brother was battling cancer. In creating the story, he was also inspired by several aspects of his life. Like the novel's main character, Steven, the author really plays the drums, he really went through an incredibly awkward year in eighth grade, and he really was completely spastic around girls until right around his twenty-first birthday. The made-up parts of the book are all reflections of the author's basic philosophy, which is that the world is a tough place, so you'd better be kind and laugh a lot.

Drums, Girls & Dangerous Pie was published to great acclaim and was named to several Best of the Year lists, including the American Library Association's Teens' Top Ten.

Steven and Jeffrey's story continues in the novel *After Ever After*. Mr. Sonnenblick is also the author of *Notes from the Midnight Driver*, which is about drunk driving, lawn gnomes, divorced parents, a unique old man, and a beautiful girl with deadly hobbies; *Zen and the Art of Faking It*, a story about one boy's attempt to fake out his entire school, escape boredom, and get the fearless, guitar-rocking girl of his dreams; and *Curveball: The Year I Lost My Grip*, about how a freak injury causes a high school pitcher to throw his life a few curves. Besides these novels, Mr. Sonnenblick has also written the Dodger and Me series for younger readers and the novel *Are You Experienced?* for older teen readers.

Mr. Sonnenblick lives in Bethlehem, Pennsylvania, with the most supportive wife and most lovable children he could ever imagine. Plus a lot of drums and guitars in the basement. You can find out a whole lot more about him at www.jordansonnenblick.com.

Note from the Author

I wrote this book for one kid. Back in 2003, when I had just finished writing the first draft, which was then titled *Steven and Jeffrey*, I decided to leave her name out of the acknowledgments and dedication. At the time, she was an eighth-grade student and I was her teacher, so I felt there were strange confidentiality issues involved with putting her name in a book. More important, she was an adolescent who was dealing with her younger brother's cancer treatment, and I didn't want to draw any attention to her or her family that might add additional stress on top of what they were already facing on a daily basis.

Several years later, I dedicated the sequel, *After Ever After*, to her, but that still didn't fully fix the problem in my head. Her name belongs in THIS book. So:

Emily Penrose.

Emily Penrose.

Emily Penrose.

It is hard to explain what Emily did for me, but I am going to try. Because in the very best moments of a teacher's career, if that teacher is extraordinarily lucky, his students become the teachers for a little while . . . and somehow, hopefully, those moments enrich the students in turn. You can't quantify it — you can't prove it with a set of test scores — but it's a thing of transcendent beauty.

So: Emily. The Girl Who Laughed. I am not going to lie. This kid drove me crazy for the first quarter of the year, because any student I put in the seat next to her immediately started talking, and Emily immediately started laughing.

Loudly.

Then I would switch around my whole seating chart, and move another kid into the space next to Emily, with the exact same result. This was a ninety-minute class, the last two periods of the day, so my patience was rather, um, thin by the end of each session. To my eternal regret, I remember yelling at Emily a lot for the first nine weeks of the year.

Then, one day, I was buying a candy bar in the main office of the school. There was a cardboard box of chocolate bars on the counter; you shoved a dollar bill down through a slot, and then reached in and grabbed your chocolate bar. I knew the candy was being sold as a fundraiser, but I hadn't stopped to wonder what the funds were for, until this one day, when the slot got jammed with bills and I had to open the box to free up the chocolate I craved. For the first time, I read the letter on the inside of the box and learned why the box was in the office. A third grader in one of the elementary schools was in treatment for cancer, and the proceeds were going to his family.

This boy's last name was the same as Emily's last name. I asked the secretary, Diane, who always knew everything, about the situation, and she told me that he was Emily's younger brother.

Emily is learning this for the first time now, from reading these pages: I walked out of that office with tears running down my face. I felt like the meanest teacher who'd ever lived. I had been yelling at this girl every day in class for laughing, when she should have been crying. Instantly, in that hallway, I had to completely revise my opinion of this girl. I had thought her laughter was a sign of immaturity, but now I decided it was actually a show of strength.

Emily, I realized, was managing to be everybody else's best friend in the middle of her family's crisis. Other kids came to her with *their* problems. If another girl ran out of class crying over a boy (which happens with alarming frequency in eighth-grade English), Emily was the one who would go after her with a handful of tissues. She could make anybody laugh. (And here's another thing I don't think Emily knew: a boy in her class used to come to me all the time with crumpled-up sheets of paper, asking me for advice about what to do with them. The pages were scrawled over with love poems about Emily.)

She was that kind of kid — kind, caring, honest, funny. Smart. Athletic. But above all, Emily was, and is, resilient. Radiantly so.

Emily was so resilient that I thought she was doing perfectly well, and said so to her mother at parent-teacher conferences. I think my exact quote was something like, "I have to tell you, I think your daughter is so brave. She's handling her brother's illness so well!" Mrs. Penrose just looked at me like I was some kind of moron and said something like, "She's not handling it well; she's *hiding* it well."

Trying not to look like a complete half-wit, I responded by asking whether it might help if I could find Emily a book to read about an eighth grader whose younger sibling was in treatment for cancer. Emily's mother liked the idea, so I went on a little English-teacher quest, but I couldn't find any books about middle schoolers whose siblings had cancer.

Confession time: When I met Emily, I was thirty-three years old, and had probably spent twenty-nine of those years bragging to anyone who would listen that I was going to write a book someday. I had written stories, songs, poetry, and plays all through my school career, and majored in English in college. However, I hadn't written anything at all since graduation — I had only boasted a lot about how I was just about to write something great.

And then there was this sweet, brave girl who needed a book that didn't exist.

I spent the first two weeks that February of Emily's eighth-grade year staying up basically all night, reading through a pile of textbooks and memoirs about cancer. Then I frantically scrawled a huge outline across five taped-together sheets of old-fashioned tractor-feed printer paper. Finally, I sat down and spent every spare waking moment of the next ten weeks writing *Steven and Jeffrey*.

Then I got bronchitis, called in sick, and slept for a week.

When I was done with the manuscript, I had one worry: What if I had made Steven too brave and too kind to his little brother, Jeffrey? Maybe people would read about the sacrifices Steven makes for Jeffrey in the novel and decide the whole story was unrealistic.

Final exam time rolled around in my class. My final was a take-home set of four essays, and that year it was due the day before grades were to be entered into the school's computer system. I warned my students repeatedly that their exams had to be in on time, or I would have to give them a failing grade. Failing my class would be a disaster, because for an eighth grader, an F meant being disqualified from the school's graduation ceremony, a spectacular affair complete with caps, gowns, and diplomas. To add insult to injury, failing a major class would mean going to summer school to make up the credit.

Emily was the first kid I ever taught who showed up at my final exam time with no essays. I took her out in the hall and asked her, as gently as I could, what had happened. She said, "My brother had to go to Philadelphia last night for blood work, and he asked me to come hold his hand."

That was when I realized I hadn't made Steven too brave or too nice to his younger brother, because this real-life person was braver and nicer, on the deepest possible level, than any character I could ever have imagined. Needless to say, I somehow finagled the system, and Emily turned in her essays a day or two after the deadline, but that's not the point. The point is that when I was a wannabe writer in search of inspiration, I was lucky enough to meet the single most inspiring kid that ever walked into Phillipsburg Middle School.

I wish the story could end there, but it doesn't. When I wrote the book, I thought I was helping Emily to deal with something that was, essentially, behind her. I believed that Emily's brother was recovering, and that I was helping her to deal with an experience that would eventually come to a positive resolution. I honestly don't think I would have had the nerve, the sheer chutzpah, to write it if I had known how badly things were actually going with his treatment.

Drums was originally published by a small press on June 1, 2004. I had already scheduled a celebratory book signing at the Phillipsburg Free Public Library, and was bursting with anticipation, when suddenly, on May 10, in the middle of the school day, the news came: Emily's brother had died.

I walked out of my classroom in the middle of silent reading and cried.

I sent Emily a card, and paid my respects, but there is very little that your eighth-grade English teacher can do for you in a situation like that. Then, twenty-one days later, Emily and several members of her extended family came to the book launch. With tears in my eyes — everyone who reads this is going to think I do nothing but type and cry! — I wrote in her copy, *To my Inspiration Girl*.

The next night, as I was cooking dinner, Mrs. Penrose called me at home, which she had never done before. My heart immediately started jackhammering in my chest, and all I could think was, "She read it! She hates it! They all hate it! What have I *done*?" I sat down heavily and stammered out, "How are you doing? What can I do for you? How is —" My memory is somewhat fuzzy on the transition here, but somehow she began complimenting me about the book, which she and Emily's father had read that day. The two lines I distinctly recall are that she said it was as though I had followed her family around the hospital with a video camera, and that I "got it right."

Can you imagine the graciousness of a woman who would make that telephone call three weeks after losing her child? I got off the telephone, stunned with gratitude. I had written the book for one kid, because I promised her mom I would find a novel about a cancer sibling, and now her mom had said I'd gotten it right.

Looking back on this story, which I have told to hundreds of thousands of people in the decade since *Drums* was published, I realize that closure never really came to me until Emily, at age twenty-three, sent me a Facebook message at the end of her first year as a student teacher. She told me that she'd never really understood how much impact a student could have on a teacher until she'd had students of her own, but that her class of third graders had changed her forever. Now she knew her life's purpose was to be a teacher. As an educator, it was my *Lion King* moment.

I am a big believer in the idea that everything we do causes ripples in the lives of the people around us, and ripples are still spreading via this book. I suppose they started with Emily's brother, Matthew John Penrose, whom I never even met, and spread through his parents, John and Martha. At the same time, of course, Emily, by being her best self every day in the midst of what could have been an absolutely paralyzing crisis, passed the ripples on to me.

So, for twelve weeks or so, because of one kid, I rose up and became my best self. I stayed up incredibly late day after day, and wrote the book I had always bragged I could write. I sent it out to the editors at a tiny publishing house. They bought the book, and printed five thousand copies, but then their company immediately went out of business. Their last, selfless act was to donate four thousand of those copies to SuperSibs!, a cancer-sibling support organization, which mailed the books for free to brothers and sisters of cancer patients all over America.

Then, through a wild coincidence, Scholastic discovered *Drums*, and published it in much greater numbers. Scholastic also made it available to SuperSibs! at an incredible discount, which enabled tens of thousands of additional cancer siblings to get copies for free. As I write this, the novel has been published in twelve foreign languages, and read by hundreds of thousands of people. More important for me, on an emotional level, are the charitable acts the book has inspired. Because the plot of the book revolves around fundraisers — an idea I got from seeing the tremendous outpouring of love and support from the town of Phillipsburg to the Penrose family — I have been privileged to visit school after school in which the students, upon reading *Drums*, have decided to partner with a local hospital and run a coin drive, a car wash, a dance-a-thon, a karaoke contest. I have watched in tears (I know! Those tears again!) on several occasions as five-figure checks have been handed over by middle-school children to the families of boys and girls in treatment. There is even a teenager in Chattanooga, Tennessee, named Jack Skowronnek who, after reading the book at age ten, started an annual head-shaving charity event called Jack's Chattanoggins. In the four years since then, Jack has raised more than $100,000 for the St. Baldrick's Foundation.

Emily showed me, by example, how to be my best self. I stepped up as well as I could. Thousands of others have followed suit, and the ripples are still moving outward.

Jordan Sonnenblick,
January 2014

Q&A with Jordan Sonnenblick

Q: *Where did you grow up? What was your family like?*

A: I was born in Fort Leonard Wood, Missouri, where my dad was stationed as an Army doctor during the Vietnam War. When I was a year old, we moved to Staten Island, New York, where I grew up, and where my mom and sister still live. I am the only member of my family who wasn't born in the five boroughs of New York City. You wouldn't think that would make a difference, but once when I was a teen-ager traveling in Canada with my sister and parents, a hotel clerk asked why I didn't have an accent like the rest of my family! There are two secret ways to unlock my dormant New York accent, though: just get me really, really mad, or put me on the phone with my best friend Jeremy, from middle school.

My parents were both highly educated: Dad was a psychi-atrist, and Mom is a dean at the City University of New York and holds a doctoral degree. My sister has a master's degree in social work. So I, with my college degree in English, am technically the least well-educated member of the family. On the other hand, I could always beat everyone except my mom at the *New York Times* crossword. In that sense, I got a lot of my English education sitting across the kitchen table from my mother, wrestling through the Sunday *Times* puzzle together.

Q: *What were you like when you were Steven's age? Were any of his band experiences or girlfriend dilemmas based on your own?*

A: Steven is totally the thirteen-year-old me, in about sev-enteen different ways. There's the drum thing, the really close female friends, the youngest-guy-in-the-band issue, and the sarcasm, for starters. Especially the sarcasm. Sadly, though, I was less cool than Steven, in some hard-to-define way. So, as a middle-schooler, I never figured out that any girl might be interested in me until far too late.

Sigh.

By the way, I love to read, so I spent a lot of my free time with books and comics in middle school. I didn't write that particular habit into Steven, for some reason. That might be the most major difference between us.

Q: *Did you always know that you wanted to be a writer? Was there a particular moment in your life that you were sure of it?*
A: I was always one of those annoying guys who say at parties, "Some day I'm going to write a novel." What finally motivated me to write *Drums* was that I met a teenage girl who I thought needed to read this particular story. Since the story only existed in my head, I finally had no choice but to get off my butt and write a book.

Q: *You spent the first part of your teaching career with Teach for America in Houston, Texas. What was that like?*
A: I loved Teach for America, and I loved Houston. My wife and I would have stayed there forever, but we wanted our children to be raised closer to their grandparents in New York City and Pennsylvania. Probably the best moment of my teaching career occurred in my fifth-grade classroom in Houston. It rarely snows there, but one day it did. All of a sudden, Maria, the quietest girl in the class, jumped over my huge desk to get to the window. I was right in the middle of teaching spelling, and I said, "Maria, sit down!

Haven't you ever seen snow before?" She said, "No, I haven't." So we cancelled the rest of the lesson and ran outside. Everyone in the class was running around, catching snowflakes on their tongues, touching the snow on each other's hair, and just generally being totally amazed by this magical moment.

W-a-y more fun than spelling, right?

Q: *What inspired you to write* Drums, Girls & Dangerous Pie?
A: As I noted above, I really wrote this book for one amazing girl. Her little brother had been battling cancer for years, and I wanted to find a book that she could relate to. When I couldn't find a novel that I felt was a good fit for her situation, I wrote one.

Q: *In the dedication you credit your son for coining "dangerous pie." What was it and how did you later link it to the story of Steven and Jeffrey?*
A: Yes, my son, Ross, gets all the credit for that one. When he was maybe three years old, he went through a cooking phase. He had this big plastic container full of toy food. One day, I was home alone with him and I heard this tremendously loud clanking from the kitchen. Running in there, I found Ross sitting on the floor, stirring a huge pot filled to the brim with all of the plastic food, about twenty Matchbox cars, a screwdriver, a wrench or two, and an entire box of penny nails — with an upside-down hammer. I asked what he was making, and he said, "Dangerous pie." How could I *not* put that in a book?

Q: *Did you have a hard time telling Jeffrey's story? What were some of the challenges and how were you able to tackle them?*

A: This story was both easy and hard for me. It was easy because the whole thing took me twelve weeks from start to finish, including research, while I was teaching full-time. So the writing was unbelievably fast. The hard part was that, if you do the math, clearly I wasn't sleeping for that quarter of a year! Also, of course, an author lives, breathes, eats, and sleeps the lives of his characters, so the sorrows of this story haunted me. Writing the book was almost an act of exorcism for me: I needed to get these people out of my head so I could rest again.

Q: *Your book is funny and also very sad, which surprises a lot of readers because we don't expect a book about cancer to be humorous as well as sad. Does it come naturally to you to see humor in all things, or did you intentionally set out to write a humorous book about cancer?*

A: I knew in advance that the book had to be funny, partly because my student was always giggling even in the midst of her real-life situation, and partly because *I* laughed my way through middle school. Truthfully, if you asked my current students, they'd tell you I am still laughing my way through middle school.

Anyway, a lot of people thought I was nuts to write a funny cancer novel — but I had to. I think one of the best and noblest things about being a human being is that we can find laughter anywhere. We just sometimes forget to look.

Q: *What is your writing routine like? Do you write every day? Do you write in a special place?*

A: I am not a routine-oriented kind of guy. Mostly, I just write late at night, until I can't keep my head up off the keyboard. Except for the last twenty pages or so of each book, which get written in a mad weekend-long spurt of insanity. Writing, for me, is like that joke: A man is walking down the street, whacking himself on the forehead with a ball-peen hammer. A woman walks up to him and says, "Doesn't that hurt?" He says, "Absolutely." The woman says, "Then why are you doing it?" The guy says, "Because it feels so good when I stop!"

So that's why my so-called "routine" for each novel is really more of a crazed dash to the finish line.

Q: *What advice would you give to aspiring writers?*

A: Sleep a lot now, while you can! No, seriously, read a ton. And don't just read one genre or format; read everything. The only way to figure out how to use the nuts and bolts of this thing called storytelling is to examine a lot of these complicated machines called books.

Q: *In addition to being a writer, you are also a seriously talented musician. Are the creation processes similar for you?*

A: I see all forms of art as being closely related. However, drumming feels great—physically great—while you're doing it, while writing only feels great afterward. The best thing about drumming is that when you're playing really, really well, you will get into a sort of trance in which you forget about everything but the beat. The best part of writing is that you get to paint pictures in other people's heads!

Q: *Do you yourself own a pair of "special sticks"?*
A: No. Probably the only object I own that I care about to that extent is a wooden anchor my father carved as a room decoration for me when I was a baby. Since my father's death in 2005, I sometimes just sit and run my fingers over the wood of the anchor and feel like I am, in some sense, spending time with my dad.

The idea for the special sticks in the novel came from my middle-school band teacher, who used to engrave each drummer's name on his or her sticks, so that we wouldn't constantly be fighting over which sticks were whose. I loved my engraved sticks, because when I was bored I could run my fingertips over the engraving and "read" my name.

I have no idea what's up with my fascination for the texture of wooden objects. So please don't ask.

Jeffrey's story continues in

Here is a sneak peek…

That first week of school had at least one other huge high-light: I met the girl of my dreams. I mean, it's not like we had some exclusive relationship or anything. She was probably the girl of just about everyone's dreams. But I'm the guy who made friends with her first.

Kind of.

It happened just before science class, first thing in the morning on the first day of school. I was trying to hustle through the crowded chaos of the hallway, which is hard to do with a limp. As I came around a corner, I saw a girl crouched down on the floor, attempting to gather up a mil-lion papers, along with the contents of her entire backpack. People were stepping around her, and even right over her stuff, but nobody was stopping to help. I figured I'd be late to class if I stopped, but I also figured this girl was going to get stampeded if someone didn't help her to pick up her stuff before the warning bell rang.

I knelt next to her and started grabbing lipsticks, packs of gum, and — uh — feminine items. Her dark hair totally covered her face, so I didn't get a look at her until we had gotten everything back together and stood up. When she looked sideways at me to say thank you, I felt my entire world shift violently on its axis. I'd heard people say that beauty can hit you suddenly, but I had thought it was a figure of speech. Uh-uh. This was like, *Ka-POW!*

Miss Ka-POW! spoke, and the torrent of words was as overwhelming as her looks. "Hey, thanks! Wow, people around here are really serious about getting to class on time. Back in California, nobody would have helped a new kid, either, but that's because they'd be worried about not looking cool. But here — geez! I felt like I was, like, in the middle of a riot. Hi, I'm Lindsey. Lindsey Abraham. We just moved here from L.A. Well, not really L.A. The O.C., technically. But close enough, right? And you're . . . ?"

I was speechless. The neurologist would tell you I have "slow processing as a late effect," which is another way of saying that people can really make me look dumb if they're quick talkers. And apparently Lindsey Abraham was, like, an intercontinental talking missile. By the time my brain worked its way through her whole train of thought, I must have looked like a total goon. "Uh, it's Jeffrey. Jeffrey Alper. From New Jersey." *Oh, good God*, I thought. *Did I really just say that?*

She giggled. "Well, hello, Jeffrey Alper from New Jersey. And thanks again for being the one person who stopped to help." The bell rang. "Ooh, now I've made you late to class."

"It's OK, my class is right here. I hope you don't think our whole school is rude. Someone would have stopped to help, but, you know, first day and all. . . ."

Lindsey Abraham smiled at me. Wow, do people have white teeth in California, or what? "It's all right. Someone *did* stop to help. By the way, are you one of those people who always see the good in everybody?"

"I try."

We looked at each other, and for that instant, we were equal — I don't think she knew what to say, either. Of course, she recovered first. "You said your class is this one, right?" She squinted at her schedule, which was partly crumpled in her hand and had a big sneaker footprint across it. "Science with, uh, Laurenzano?"

"Yeah, but watch out going in. He's famous for getting mad when people come in late."

Lindsey smiled again. *I could get used to that smile*, I thought. On second thought, no, I'd probably never get used to it. I liked it, though. A lot. "Come with me," she said. "I owe you one. Is that the back door of this room? OK, you hit that one, and I'll go in the front." Then she turned on her heel and barged into the room like it was a Hollywood party and she was on the red carpet. I headed for the back door. What else was I going to do?